SHIPMENT ONE

Tex Times Ten by Tina Leonard
Runaway Cowboy by Judy Christenberry
Crazy for Lovin' You by Teresa Southwick
The Rancher Next Door by Cathy Gillen Thacker
Intimate Secrets by B.J. Daniels
Operation: Texas by Roxanne Rustand

SHIPMENT TWO

Navarro or Not by Tina Leonard
Trust a Cowboy by Judy Christenberry
Taming a Dark Horse by Stella Bagwell
The Rancher's Family Thanksgiving by Cathy Gillen Thacker
The Valentine Two-Step by RaeAnne Thayne
The Cowboy and the Bride by Marin Thomas

SHIPMENT THREE

Catching Calhoun by Tina Leonard
The Christmas Cowboy by Judy Christenberry
The Come-Back Cowboy by Jodi O'Donnell
The Rancher's Christmas Baby by Cathy Gillen Thacker
Baby Love by Victoria Pade
The Best Catch in Texas by Stella Bagwell
This Kiss by Teresa Southwick

SHIPMENT FOUR

Archer's Angels by Tina Leonard
More to Texas than Cowboys by Roz Denny Fox
The Rancher's Promise by Jodi O'Donnell
The Gentleman Rancher by Cathy Gillen Thacker
Cowboy's Baby by Victoria Pade
Having the Cowboy's Baby by Stella Bagwell

SHIPMENT FIVE

Belonging to Bandera by Tina Leonard
Court Me, Cowboy by Barbara White Daille
His Best Friend's Bride by Jodi O'Donnell
The Cowboy's Return by Linda Warren
Baby Be Mine by Victoria Pade
The Cattle Baron by Margaret Way

SHIPMENT SIX

Crockett's Seduction by Tina Leonard
Coming Home to the Cattleman by Judy Christenberry
Almost Perfect by Judy Duarte
Cowboy Dad by Cathy McDavid
Real Cowboys by Roz Denny Fox
The Rancher Wore Suits by Rita Herron
Falling for the Texas Tycoon by Karen Rose Smith

SHIPMENT SEVEN

Last's Temptation by Tina Leonard
Daddy by Choice by Marin Thomas
The Cowboy, the Baby and the Bride-to-Be by Cara Colter
Luke's Proposal by Lois Faye Dyer
The Truth About Cowboys by Margot Early
The Other Side of Paradise by Laurie Paige

SHIPMENT EIGHT

Mason's Marriage by Tina Leonard
Bride at Briar's Ridge by Margaret Way
Texas Bluff by Linda Warren
Cupid and the Cowboy by Carol Finch
The Horseman's Son by Delores Fossen
Cattleman's Bride-to-Be by Lois Faye Dyer

The rugged, masculine and independent men
of America's West know the value of hard work,
honor and family. They may be ranchers, tycoons
or the guy next door, but they're all cowboys at heart.
Don't miss any of the books in this collection!

Cowboy
at
Heart

CRAZY FOR LOVIN' YOU

TERESA SOUTHWICK

HARLEQUIN®
entertain, enrich, inspire™

Recycling programs
for this product may
not exist in your area.

ISBN-13: 978-0-373-82604-9

CRAZY FOR LOVIN' YOU

Copyright © 2001 by Teresa Ann Southwick

www.Harlequin.com

Printed in U.S.A.

TERESA SOUTHWICK

lives with her husband in Las Vegas, the city that reinvents itself every day. An avid fan of romance novels, she is delighted to be living out her dream of writing for Harlequin.

To my agent, Linda Kruger, for your support, encouragement and exceptional organizational skills. Thanks for always being there.

Prologue

"Go 'way, kid."

"But, Mitch—"

"I don't want to see or talk to anyone named Stevens."

Taylor Stevens stared at the dark expression on Mitch Rafferty's face and wondered what had happened and how fast she could change her name. Her sister must have done something. Only Jen could put Mitch's nose out of joint like this.

If only he would notice her instead, Taylor thought dejectedly. She might be younger than he, but she was more mature than he thought. Certainly old enough to notice his sandy-brown hair, his broad shoulders that made all the girls sit up and take notice, and those bad-boy blue eyes. Especially his eyes. Whenever he looked at her, her heart beat so hard she got a little scared.

The Texas state high school rodeo championships in Abilene had just ended. Tomorrow they would go home to Destiny. It was their last night at the Lamplighter Motel and she'd found Mitch by the pool. She took a deep breath and a heaping dose of courage as she sat down on the lounge chair next to his.

Other teenagers sat nearby, but didn't seem to be paying any attention to her and Mitch. He looked like a volcano about to erupt and she was afraid for him. Afraid of what he might do. She just couldn't leave him alone. The feelings she had for him were so deep, so big she felt she might burst any second.

Taylor touched his arm, then started when he flinched away. "Okay. Don't look at me. Just tell me what's wrong, then listen while I talk."

"Get lost, kid," he growled. "Don't you get it? I don't want you here. I want to be alone."

Kid? She wanted to grab his shirtfront and show him she was no kid. In fact, she would pit her fourteen years against his nineteen any day of the week and twice on Sunday.

She took a deep breath. "You're acting like someone took away your favorite toy. At least tell me why. What's wrong? I thought we were friends."

"... and I are through." The smoldering ... n his eyes hinted that there was more.

But all he said was "I could never be friends with anyone related to her."

Taylor's first thought was stunned disbelief that her sister was dumb enough to let a guy like Mitch go. Her second: she was going to hell for being so happy that he was no longer spoken for.

"I'm sorry," she said lamely, not meeting his gaze in the dim light surrounding the pool. If he looked at her, he would know she wasn't sorry at all.

Silence stretched between them. It was late and everyone else who was at the motel had turned in. Or almost everyone. Behind her, she could hear the kids around the pool talking, and muffled voices and giggles beyond the shrubs that shielded her and Mitch. On the far sidewalk, a guy with a square competition number attached to his long-sleeved Western shirt walked hand in hand with a girl Taylor recognized from the rodeo week queen's court. Crickets chirped and the muted sound of television drifted to them from nearby rooms.

"I'm really sorry," she said again. And she truly did feel bad that he was hurting so. When he remained silent, she added, "But she's not the only girl on the planet, Mitch."

"She is for me."

Taylor cared about him more than her sister ever could. Why couldn't he see that? How could he not know that he was the first person she thought about in the morning and the last one to cross her mind before sleep took her at night? Every waking second in between, she wished she were with him, just to be in his presence, just to look at him.

Mitch had brushed her off the night before, when she'd tried to tag along with him to the lake. But now she knew he wasn't going steady with her sister. Taylor knew it might be her best chance to make him notice her.

"What about me?" she blurted out, unable to hold back any longer. "*I* love you. *I'd* never hurt you. Not in a million years."

Maybe if she showed him. Before she could think it over, she leaned forward and touched her mouth to his. She tasted surprise and hesitation in his unyielding mouth. Then he pulled back and stared at her. The look in his eyes made her wish she could take it all back—especially the kiss. Or better yet, if only a twister would swoop out of nowhere and dump her in Kansas so she wouldn't have to see that bitter, cold expression on his face. He stood up, inches from the deep end of the pool. She stood, too, because he towered over her and she didn't like him looking down at her.

"You kiss like a little girl."

She heard laughter behind her. Her cheeks were hot with embarrassment, but it was nothing compared to the pain just starting to seep into her heart.

He folded his arms over his chest. "Even if I hadn't sworn off women, you've got three strikes against you."

"Like what?" she asked before she could stop herself.

"You're her sister. That kiss proves you're a baby. And you're skinny as a—"

"I know I'm not pretty," she interrupted, not wanting the words to come from him. He'd just rubbed salt in an open wound. "I'm not pretty *yet*. But you just wait, Mitch Rafferty. I'll show you."

Without thinking, Taylor put her hands on his chest and shoved for all she was worth. He went backward into the pool, his cold expression changing to one of stunned surprise just before he went under. She turned but she knew he'd surfaced behind her. The spluttering was a big clue.

She walked away before he could see that the moisture on her cheeks had nothing to do with the splash his big body had made. With every step, she vowed she *would* show him if it was the last thing she ever did.

Chapter One

Ten years later...

Mitch Rafferty was back in town.

And she was going to see him any minute. Taylor Stevens looked out her living room window wondering if he would be on time. As the newly appointed commissioner of the high school rodeo association, it was his job to find a site for the state championships. It was an event she desperately wanted. When she'd found out Mitch was the man who held her future in his hands, she'd been stunned. Even now she wondered which of the gods she'd offended and how she could make amends.

She needed him to pick her—or rather her ranch, the Circle S. She had a lot riding on this. But if history repeated itself, she was in a lot of trouble.

The sound of a car engine drifted to her

over the hum of the central air-conditioning in the house. She cracked the shutter in the front room enough to peek out. The late-model, extended-cab pickup crunching rocks and dirt as it came to a halt in her circular driveway was unfamiliar. Her stomach dropped; he was here.

Ever since finding out Mitch was back, she'd been as nervous as a small kitten up a big tree. And not only because he could impact her life. Over and over she'd repeated to herself that she didn't care about him anymore. She was a big girl now and he couldn't hurt her.

Tell that to her hammering heart.

She turned away and took a deep breath as she brushed her hands down her khaki slacks, then adjusted the belt, at the same time making sure her buttercup-yellow blouse was neatly tucked in. No point in meeting him wearing the dirty jeans and work shirt she'd worn to muck out stalls that morning. She might be country, but she cleaned up pretty good and wanted to put her best boot forward.

There was a knock on the door and she took a deep breath as she counted to ten. Heaven forbid she looked too anxious.

"Here goes nothing," she said, opening the door wide.

Her heart nearly stopped. Mitch was a decade older, but he looked even better than she remembered. His eyes were still bad-boy blue and hinted of mischief. His hair was the same sandy-brown, and his well-formed nose crooked enough to keep him from being too perfect. The angular face and square jaw were somehow more rugged. Why did she find that so incredibly appealing?

Right there on her front porch stood Mitch Rafferty, the same man who had two-stepped on her tender fourteen-year-old heart. Shock sanded ten years away. Feelings that were every bit as big and deep and painful as they'd been that night engulfed her again. She wished she didn't remember, but she did. All too clearly.

The humiliation of their last encounter washed over her as it had countless times since. It had become the standard by which she judged all disasters. She'd said *way* too much. Followed by a kiss that even with a decade in between made her cheeks burn now. She couldn't seem to form a coherent thought, let alone get a word past the Texas-size lump in her throat.

He looked at her for several moments before recognition jumped into his gaze. "Taylor?"

"Mitch. It's been a long time."

No kidding. It had taken him several moments to know her. But she'd been a skinny kid the last time they'd seen each other. He'd told her she kissed like a little girl. If there was any cosmic justice, she would *not* blush at that thought. She was a grown woman now, not the kid who'd pushed him into the pool. The memory had dominated her recollections ever since learning he was the new commissioner.

Would he hold it against her? Even worse, would he recall how she'd bared her soul?

When her silence dragged on, he cleared his throat. "How have you been?"

"Fine. You?" she asked.

"Great."

"Did you just get into town?" she asked.

He nodded. "I drove in from El Paso this morning." He continued to stare at her. "*You* look great."

"Skinny little me?" she asked, unable to resist the jab, testing the waters, so to speak. Then she smiled, hoping the nerves line-dancing in her stomach didn't make her mouth quiver. "You don't have to say that, Mitch."

"I mean it. You've really changed," he said,

grinning his good-ol'-boy grin, the one that showed his even, white teeth to perfection.

It was also the one that told her he said something equally flirtatious to all the girls. Although she'd tried to forget about him, over the years she hadn't escaped reading about him in tabloid and magazine stories that had touted the sexy bull rider's athletic and romantic conquests. Before dropping out of sight, he'd been linked to women she could never compete with. Why would he remember that they'd once been friends?

"You've grown up."

"That happens in—" She paused for what she hoped was just the right thoughtful expression. "How long has it been? When did I last see you?"

Fiddledeedee, she wanted to say in her best Scarlett O'Hara voice. If God was *her* witness, Mitch would never know that she clearly remembered the last time she'd seen him he'd been going backward into the deep end of the pool.

"I can't say. And I try not to think back too far." For just a second, a frown chased away the mischief in his eyes. "Offhand I'd say it's been a long time because I haven't been back to Destiny for ten or eleven years."

"That long?" she said with as much innocence as she could dredge up.

He nodded. "Give or take. These days I feel like I've been rode hard and put up wet."

Just these days? He'd been wet the last time she'd seen him. But right this minute, she thought he looked awfully good. Better than good. In fact, better than he had ten years ago. That wasn't supposed to happen. Wasn't his hairline supposed to recede? Not only *didn't* he have forty square miles of forehead, but his hair was thick and she couldn't detect a single gray hair in the sandy color. It was cut conservatively short. She knew it would curl with a bit more length.

A man his age should have at least the beginnings of a beer gut. He had to be pushing thirty. Surely his belly had gone doughy. But one glance at his white shirt tucked into the waistband of his soft, worn Wranglers confirmed that his abdomen was washboard firm. And his long sleeves were rolled up to just below his elbows, right where she thought a man's sleeves ought to be. It was a look that got her every time.

Okay. Get a grip. There was some good news. She was no longer a lovesick fourteen-year-old. She didn't care about him anymore. They would probably touch on her embarrassing confession of ten years ago followed by that impulsive kiss, chalk it up to high school hormones, then forget about it.

"So you don't remember the last time we saw each other?" she asked, fishing to find out what, if anything, he recalled.

"Should I?" He looked thoughtful.

"I guess not."

He didn't remember. Wasn't that good news? Then why was she flirting with annoyance that her all-around most humiliating moment wasn't important enough for him to store in his memory?

He shook his head. "All I can say is you've really changed."

"I'll take that as a compliment."

"I almost didn't recognize you. Your hair is different."

Of course he would remember her long, straight, unflattering mousey-brown hair. After two years at Texas A&M, her roommate had helped her find a flattering hairstyle and shown her that lipstick was good for more than writing messages on the bathroom mirror. Finally Taylor had taken her first step in the struggle to repair the confidence that a few moments with Mitch had destroyed. And her social life had soared from there. Right until a year ago when her fiancé dumped her for the woman who had once dumped him. That had reminded her how fragile her confidence truly was.

Mitch studied her thoroughly. Was there an appreciative sparkle in his eyes? Was that a glow spreading through her? A direct reaction to his subtle but nice words? Doggone it! She thought she'd prepared herself for him. Why could he still get to her? She'd worked so hard to nurture a spine along with her self-esteem. Two minutes facing Mitch Rafferty, once known as Texas's most eligible cowboy, and the glow he generated threatened to melt her backbone into slush.

She realized he was still on the porch. "I didn't mean to keep you standing out there. Please come in. Where are my manners?"

In the manure heap along with her self-confidence.

His boots rang on the wooden floor as he stepped inside. "Thanks."

One word, just a single syllable, but uttered in his deep voice and it was enough to shake her up as surely as a tumble from a stubborn horse.

She shut the door, closing out the beginning of May warmth. It wasn't hot yet, not like it would get in August. But she'd set the inside thermostat to keep the interior comfortable.

She didn't want to give him any reason to thumbs-down her ranch for the event. Getting even with her would be reason enough. But only if he remembered and knew how much she was counting on a go-ahead.

He stood in the entryway, sliding his black Stetson through his hands as he looked around. A frown drew his eyebrows together. What was he thinking? she wondered. Her glance swept the area. To her right was the living room with the flagstone fireplace that dominated the large square area. Two blue-and-green-plaid love seats, with a simple oak coffee table between, sat in front of it.

To her left was what her family had always called the parlor, also with a large fireplace, this time brick, and a new, expensive, state-of-the-art reclining sectional in front of a big-screen TV. Beyond that was the dining room and the kitchen. The dark wood floor extended throughout all the rooms on the first floor. The house had been built in the 1930s and the land it stood on had been in the family for several generations. The money she'd spent on new furnishings was part of her plan to see it stayed that way.

"How's Jen?" he asked.

She should have known he was remembering the other member of her own generation.

Her sister. Before she could prevent it, there was a dull pain right near her heart. "Jensen is fine. She works in Dallas," she added.

Best let him know up front that he wouldn't be seeing a lot of her. At least not in Destiny. In case that was why he'd come back.

"A lawyer?" he asked.

"She specializes in family law."

She tried like crazy not to let it bother her that he remembered Jensen had always talked about becoming a lawyer. No doubt they'd told each other all their hopes and dreams. He'd barely recognized her, but remembered that Jensen had always wanted to be an attorney. Even though she'd broken his heart by eloping with someone else. Did he still not want to see or talk to anyone named Stevens?

"So what have you been up to for the last ten or eleven years?" she asked to fill the silence.

His gaze settled on her. "Rodeo. At first."

"I heard you gave up your scholarship."

"Seemed like the thing to do at the time." He frowned and the thundercloud expression on his face took her back to that night by the pool.

She wanted to bite her tongue. In all these years, she hadn't managed to activate the mechanism in her brain that would refine or remove anything stupid on the way to her mouth. Or maybe it was Mitch Rafferty who deactivated it. She never could think straight around him.

Nervously she tucked a bothersome strand of hair behind her ear. "Why don't we go into the kitchen? Can I get you a glass of iced tea?"

"I'd like that."

She held out her hand for him to go first and he found his way as surely as if he'd been there only yesterday. She hated herself for noticing that the back of him was almost as impressive as the front. Broad shoulders tapered to his trim waist. His backside, hugged by impossibly soft and worn denim, was practically a work of art. And that was strictly objective female appreciation for an above-average-looking man. Because she had no feelings for him whatsoever.

But when her hormones subsided, she noticed that he limped slightly. She recalled reading a small blurb about an injury, but the celebrity magazine articles mostly proclaimed that his playboy points matched his impressive rodeo stats. Was there more to his story? Probably. The fact that he was acting commissioner of the high school rodeo association was a clue.

The fact that she wanted to hear every last detail just made her a candidate for crazy. She needed him to look at the ranch and tell her it would work just fine for his purposes. Then she prayed that he would go away and never come back. But she'd opened her mouth and offered him iced tea. Taking back the offer probably wasn't the best strategy to win friends and influence people.

The kitchen was arranged in a large U, part of which formed a bar with stools. Instead of sitting on one of them the way he'd always done, he invaded her work space inside the U, parking himself with his back propped against the beige ceramic-tile counter. She felt his gaze on her as she pulled the pitcher of iced tea from the refrigerator beside the stove and opened the cupboard above to retrieve a glass.

More memories came flooding back as she poured the amber-colored liquid and handed it to him, not easy to do with trembling hands. She'd poured him iced tea all those times she'd kept him company while he'd waited for Jen to come downstairs. She tried to clamp the lid tight on the details but failed miserably at forgetting how she'd pined for him, hoping and fantasizing that a miracle would happen and he would notice *her*. That someday he would wait downstairs for *her* to get ready to go out with him.

"How did you wind up in charge of the high school rodeo association?" she asked. "It wouldn't have anything to do with the fact that you were once the state bull-riding champion, would it?"

"You remember that?"

"Yeah, I do."

A muscle in his jaw contracted for a moment before he continued, "As you pointed out, I gave up my scholarship to join the pro rodeo circuit. I did okay that first year, although I wasn't the overall point winner. But I took nationals in Wyoming. I was nineteen. It was a sign to make hay while the sun shines, so to speak."

"Then what?"

"I rode the crest for two or three years until—"

"Until what?" she encouraged.

"I had a couple of injuries," he said as if it was no big deal.

She decided to mimic his tone and keep it light. "Really? Imagine that. Riding a ton or two of ticked-off bull is hardly more challenging than a merry-go-round at the Texas state fair," she teased.

One corner of his mouth lifted. "Yeah" was

all he said. "All the hits were to my right leg. The third injury was bad. The doc said one more and I might never walk again—at least not on my own two feet."

The words tugged at her heart in spite of all her warnings to harden it. She knew how much rodeo had meant to him. It was all he'd talked about. "Oh, Mitch, I had no idea. I didn't mean to—"

He held up his hand. "It's okay. I managed to take it in stride," he said with a grin. "Pardon the pun."

His smile kicked the butterflies in her stomach into fluttering again. She thought she'd reined them in. Apparently that was something else she'd been wrong about.

"That still leaves out a couple steps—pardon the pun," she said.

His grin widened. "I went back to school."

"But your scholarship?"

He shook his head. "I didn't need it then. Not like—"

He stopped, but she knew what he'd almost said. In high school he'd been a poor kid in a foster home until the state turned him loose at eighteen. Then he'd been on his own and needed that scholarship if he wanted a chance at a higher education. That was why she'd been so stunned when he gave it up.

"So you went to college?" She leaned back against the counter and folded her arms over her chest. A large space separated them, but it wasn't enough to blunt the force of his appeal. Or the way he could stir up her emotions without even trying.

"Yeah." He set his tea on the ceramic tile beside him. "I got my degree in business from UCLA. Then I started R&R Development."

"I've heard of it," she said. The only thing she hadn't heard was that he owned it.

"You have?"

She nodded. "I read the business section of the paper every day. Your company has been mentioned a couple of times for projects pending here in Texas. By all accounts it's a company to watch."

"I'm working on it," he said. "But I missed the rodeo."

"Who wouldn't? Everyone should be stomped into the dirt by an angry bull at least once a day."

She couldn't help laughing and he joined her. Rewind ten years—to before everything had gone wrong. That was how she felt. Putty in his hands. For just an instant. Just until she shut it down cold. She didn't ever want to go there again. She was through loving men who loved someone else.

"How did you get sucked into volunteering?" she asked.

"That's an interesting choice of words."

Not really, she wanted to say. He was young, a hunk and a half, so many buckle bunnies, so little time. She wanted to say she knew him, at least she had. Ten years ago he was a loner who didn't play well with others. The high school coaches had courted him for team sports but he'd turned them down flat in favor of bull riding. But she didn't say anything. She just looked at him.

"Okay." He crossed one booted foot over the other as he continued to lean against the tiled countertop. "Dev Hart called me."

"Really?"

Dev had a ranch in Destiny and had taken over the stock business from his father. He supplied animals to rodeos all over the country. He and Mitch had rodeoed together in high school. She and Dev were friends.

"Yeah. We've kept in touch. The association was in a real bind when the commissioner resigned. Work and family obligations, he said. I don't have those." He let the sentence hang there. "Dev thought I might be interested in helping out. Since I have business dealings in the area."

So he wasn't married. All the willpower in

the world couldn't prevent her insides from doing the dance of joy. But she got the feeling there was more, a still deeper reason. "And?"

"He put the bite on me. It's no big deal, just temporary. I wouldn't have agreed to a permanent position."

"Dev must have had some clue that you would even consider doing it."

"I guess he did."

"So what was it?"

"He knew rodeo saved my life."

Mitch wasn't sure what had made him say that, especially when he saw the surprised look on Taylor's face. She tried to hide it, and he found it amazingly appealing that she couldn't.

There was something about being back in Destiny. More specifically back in this room with Taylor Stevens. He'd been telling the truth when he'd said that he'd hardly known her at first. She *had* changed—in all the right places. Her light brown hair was shoulder-length and the layers were streaked with gold highlights. Brown eyes full of spirit and intelligence challenged him. She'd been just a kid the last time he'd seen her. That night—

The longer he stood in this kitchen, back on the Circle S, talking to Jen's little sister, the more he remembered. Feelings washed over him—frustration, yearning, anger that burned into rage and a feeling of helplessness that he rode like a broken-in saddle.

"Saved your life?"

"You know as well as I do that I was a kid no one wanted." *Not even your sister,* he thought. "I could have gone either way."

"I know your background."

"That's a polite way of saying my father walked out before I took my first breath on earth, and my mother took off with a construction worker when I was ten."

"I bet no one's used that nickname in a long time."

"Riffraff?"

Why was she bringing all this up? he thought angrily. Taylor already knew and he'd spent all his life trying to live that down. Didn't make any damn sense.

"That's the one. It's ancient history," she said, completely unimpressed.

He almost smiled. "Not to me. It's who I am. But I've come to terms with it." That was only half a lie. "But back then, bull riding was all I had. I was good at it."

"You were the only person I knew who was meaner and madder than those bulls."

He grinned. "Back then I had reason to be. But I learned some important lessons."

When he didn't elaborate, she said, "Don't keep me in suspense. What did you learn?"

"Don't nod your head unless you mean it."

"A bull rider's number one rule, you used to say."

"I'm surprised you remember that."

She lifted one shoulder. "I have a good memory."

Unlike him, he finished for her. There wasn't much good to remember about that time. Which brought him to his other favorite rule. "I found out there's something more important than that."

"Which is?" she asked.

"Don't count on anyone but yourself."

He saw the shadow that crossed her pretty face and wondered about it. But not enough to ask. He wasn't here to get reacquainted. Although he didn't remember that intriguing indentation in her chin. And he couldn't help thinking how much fun it would be to explore.

"I don't think you learned the right lesson," she said. "Who taught you that?"

"Your sister. Rodeo week. The night I found her having sex with Zach Adams, who just happened to be the overall point winner at the state championships."

Chapter Two

"I didn't know you'd found out about them like that," she said, her already big eyes growing wider.

Mitch looked around the kitchen, anywhere but at the shocked expression on Taylor's face. When he finally met her gaze, his irritation dissolved just enough to let a little guilt seep in. He'd wanted to shock her, he realized. *Why?* Because she reminded him of everything he'd worked so hard to forget? Including his shabby background? If that was the case, he'd sunk to a new low. Or was he just living up to Destiny's low expectations? It really didn't matter. The truth was out and he couldn't say he was sorry—except about Taylor. There was something still innocent about her.

But he'd thought her sister was, too, and she'd thrown him over for another guy. Why would Taylor be any different? Not that it mattered. Because he wasn't looking. But something about her appealed to him. For that reason alone, he reminded himself to watch out for her.

Still, it was a stretch for him to believe Taylor hadn't known about him finding the lovers in Zach's car. The two sisters had always been as thick as thieves. Although he didn't remember much about Taylor, his gut told him she wasn't that good an actress.

"Jen didn't tell you how we broke up?" he asked.

"I didn't know about her and Zach until after they'd eloped." Her dark eyes were sad and angry at the same time.

He casually lifted one shoulder. "How did your father take it?"

"Better than I expected."

"So I came in a distant second with father and daughter."

Her gaze shot to his. "She didn't plan it, Mitch. It just happened. She fell head over heels in love and—"

"And stepped on anyone who stood in her way," he finished. He didn't care about Jen anymore. Why was he rehashing this? To push Taylor away? There was no need to do that. She was a member of Destiny's founding family, and her father had made it clear that he hated Mitch's guts. Or at least the fact that Jen liked him. Taylor probably shared her father's conviction and had a low opinion of him.

"Jen would never have deliberately deceived you." A shadow clouded her face. "I think it all happened fast and she couldn't bring herself to hurt you. I know my sister. I know how badly she felt."

"Then it's real hard for me to believe you didn't know about them."

And didn't tell me, he silently added.

"Are you calling me a liar?"

"Is your last name Stevens?"

"No one set out to make a fool of you, Mitch."

Whether he believed her or not, the fact remained that it happened ten years ago. He hadn't thought about Jen in a long time. What was it about coming back to Destiny that churned everything up again?

"You're right. I apologize." He rubbed a hand across his neck.

"That first year on the rodeo circuit must have been hard on you," she said. "Seeing Jen and Zach all the time."

The last thing he wanted was her pity. "Only because I came in second." She opened her mouth to say something and he jumped in.

"The competition was good for publicity. They milked it for all it was worth."

"Until Zach was killed." Her gaze searched his face. "Were you there?"

He shook his head. "I was sitting that one out. A pulled muscle." But he'd heard. He'd tried to contact Jen. But he'd missed her or she hadn't wanted to talk to him. Either way, it was a long time ago.

"She got her life together and moved forward." Taylor released a huge sigh. "But they had so little time together. It's so unfair."

Unfair? No kidding. But he could give lessons in unfair. The woman he'd believed was his had tossed him aside for his rival. Ten years ago, Jen had done what she'd had to. That was that. He'd gotten over her. Only one other time had he taken a chance. Another big mistake. These days he made it a point not to let down his guard for any woman, and there was no reason to relax it now.

He glanced around the kitchen and noted the copper cow trivet just to Taylor's left on the counter. The black-and-white bovine teakettle resting on the cooktop. Feminine touches were everywhere. Homey touches. Emptiness kicked up inside him like rheumatism on a damp, cold day.

"I learned something else you might want

to think about," he said more sharply than he intended.

"What's that?"

"Life isn't fair. And folks don't much care about fair. They make their minds up, and nothing short of an act of God will change it. They pretty much assume the fruit doesn't fall far from the tree. And my family tree didn't have any fruit—except for me. Or roots, either, for that matter. Your dad reminded me of that on a pretty regular basis."

"I know. But I can tell you're not bitter," she said, then bit her lip to stifle a smile.

"Of course not."

The corners of his mouth turned up and the movement felt rusty. He'd forgotten how she could do that, even at fourteen. She was even better now. In just a few words she'd pointed out what an idiot he was making of himself and made him smile at the same time.

"You're right about Dad," she said. "But it probably wouldn't do any good to say I'm sorry."

"Nope. It was a long time ago." He folded his arms over his chest. "It's water under the bridge."

"Is it?" she asked. "With Jen, too?" She looked as if his answer meant a lot to her.

"Yeah. I'm not the same green kid. And

you said Jen's moved forward. Now that she's married, probably with a couple kids—"

Taylor shook her head. "There hasn't been anyone else—since Zach."

"That's hard to believe."

"As pretty as she is?" she asked. Without waiting for an answer, she continued. "She was busy with college and law school, then her career. But I think it's more than that. She's a one-man woman." There was an edge to her voice, as if she was trying to convince him of the fact.

"Are you a one-man woman, too?"

Her cheeks flooded with color and her gaze lowered to his shirt collar. "We're not talking about me."

"But we could."

She shook her head. "No. I'd rather talk about you."

He nodded. He had nothing to lose by laying his cards on the table. "Okay. After Jen I moved on."

"I know." Her gaze didn't quite settle on his. "I still remember the stuff in the media. How did it feel to be on the Most Eligible Cowboy in Texas list? A buckle bunny in every port?"

"I think that's the navy. And don't believe everything you read," he warned her.

The tension in her body said she wanted to climb back in the saddle and ride that one until she'd gentled it. But he wasn't going there. He was a bachelor, but definitely not eligible. He'd once heard nothing was as bad as your first love gone south. The hurt of it was something you never forgot. Jen was smart, beautiful, socially accepted, the kind of woman a guy like him wasn't supposed to have. And he'd found out he couldn't have her.

"I'm glad Jen's okay. I wish her all the best in her life," he said. "I don't hold a grudge, Taylor."

"I'm glad," she said fervently. "I wish my dad could see you now. What a success you are."

Would he be such a success if Zach had lived? He liked to think the rivalry made them both better and that he would have beaten Zach Adams. The only thing he'd ever wanted was to be number one, fair and square. Now he would never know.

"I heard your dad passed away."

She nodded. "Heart attack. A little over a year ago."

"I'm sorry."

She nodded. "He wasn't a hard man. In fact just the opposite."

"If you say so."

"He just had trouble showing his feelings. Even with Jen and me. It was his way of building character. But he never missed a school or sporting event. I don't think he disliked rodeo as much as he worried about me participating."

"You knew him better than I did."

"You're right. And he would be glad you're so successful."

"Yeah. And pigs can fly," he scoffed.

"It's true. In fact, you remind me a lot of him."

"Them's fightin' words," he said.

She cocked her head to the side and her eyes twinkled. "Did you just make a joke?"

"If it gets out, I'll deny it. And wherever he is, I don't think your dad would take kindly to your comparing me to him. You'll be dodging lightning bolts if you're not careful."

"Go ahead. Make fun of me. But he wasn't a man to let on that he cared about the people in his life. It was only okay to be openly emotional about the ranch. I think you hide your softer side like that, too."

"I used to. When I was younger. But I had a lot to prove back then."

She slid him a speculative, appraising look. "So what does your softer side care about?"

"Like I said—rodeo." It was safe to care about that. It was business and only as personal as he cared to get about anything.

"So you're not really back to prove something?" she asked, looking as if she could see something he couldn't.

He shook his head. "I'm here to make sure there are championships. That's all."

He still wasn't sure why he'd agreed to Dev's suggestion that he fill in as commissioner. He'd meant to say no, and the next thing he knew, he'd agreed.

"Obviously you know I'm interested in having it here?"

He nodded. "Dev Hart told me. We've kept in touch. I suppose *you* already know that he took over the stock business from his dad."

Taylor nodded. "We still feed and take care of some of his rodeo animals."

"That's right," he said, feeling as if a video in his head was replaying pictures. More to himself than her, he said, "I used to work at the gas station in town to earn the ten bucks a ride your dad charged to let me practice on the bulls. That's how I first met your sister," he added, then kicked himself.

He thought he'd forgotten all that. Was it the familiar surroundings bringing it all back?

"So what did you and Dev talk about?" she

asked, ignoring the personal and turning the conversation back to business.

Fine with him, Mitch thought. He needed to end this stroll down memory lane. "Dev supplies prime stock to local rodeos as well as events all over the country. When I asked him if he had any suggestions for a site to hold the championships, he suggested the Circle S. I have to admit I was surprised—until I heard about your dad's passing. He wasn't a big rodeo supporter."

"That's not completely true. He raised stock to sell for the events. He just wasn't happy about me barrel racing. Watching me compete took him away from the ranch."

He grinned as a memory flashed into his mind. "You were the quickest little thing I ever saw. Fourteen seconds the last time I saw you ride."

"I never raced again after that."

"Why not? You had so much potential."

"As you said, I didn't have my dad's support." Her frown said there was more, but she closed up tighter than the chute after the bull got out.

"I'm surprised you remembered my time."

No more than he was. He'd suppressed almost everything that happened back then. But now memories—about her—were surfacing in spite of himself. She'd been a kid back then. But she was all grown up now. And pretty. Too pretty for his peace of mind.

"Your time was the same as your age," he said.

"I'm impressed," she commented, looking anything but. In fact she looked as if she was waiting for the other shoe to fall. "Memory by association. Good technique."

"Is that flattery?"

"Heaven forbid. Your ego's twice the size of Texas now."

He laughed, charmed by her straight talk. He'd had enough insincere compliments to last a lifetime. Women came on to him, wanting to hang around for their own selfish reasons. "About the rodeo—"

She leaned back against the counter on the other side of the room. "So Dev told you I'd be interested?"

He nodded. "Said you've got a project in the works and it would help you out." He'd been real curious when he'd heard that.

"You already know the ranch," she said, nodding. "Why do you have to inspect it?"

A good question. His first instinct had been to look elsewhere. But he owed it to the hardworking rodeo kids to find the best location to showcase their talents.

"My memories of the Circle S are from ten years ago, when I was just a kid. I need to see that you can handle the crowd, the animals. That the facilities are in good shape. There's a lot more to it than putting out the date and time. We have equipment, vendors, supplies, not to mention a budget."

She smiled. "Spoken like a genuine businessman."

"If the boot fits—" He shrugged.

Her smile lit up her face like the town square at Christmas. His responding flash of heat took him by surprise. She was so the girl-next-door, kid-sister type. But there was something about her, something different from the sketchy details he remembered.

He studied her more closely. Brown eyes warm and welcoming as expensive brandy looked bigger and more beautiful than he recalled. Her face had softened into a woman's, along with her body. She was still small, but she'd filled out in all the right places. The cotton shirt she wore emphasized the shape and size of her breasts. She wasn't stacked like the groupies who had pursued him on the circuit, but she would fit a man's hands perfectly. She would fit his hands—

He shut the gate on that thought before it had time to form. How she would feel was on a need-to-know basis and he didn't need to know.

But he couldn't stop himself from looking. He continued his assessment to her trim waist in khaki slacks that showed off her slender legs. He couldn't help wondering how she would look in a worn pair of jeans, soft enough to caress her backside like a lover's hand. He would put money on the fact that she could have every guy in a crowd slack-jawed and bug-eyed. Just an impartial, impersonal observation. Nothing more. She was a woman any man would be proud to have by his side.

Any man but him.

"Would you like me to show you around, or do you want to check out the place on your own?" she asked.

After the thoughts he'd just had, he would be nuts to accept her offer. Common sense told him to go it by himself as he always did. But before he could get the right words out, he heard himself say, "I think it would be helpful if you gave me the tour."

Helpful to whom? Beneficial to what? Certainly not him. Women had been kicking him in the teeth since he was ten years old. He would much rather have done business with Taylor's father. At least the man was up-front about the way things were. No surprises. God, Mitch hated surprises.

"Okay," she said. "My truck is in back."

"Let's take mine," he countered.

"Are you one of those guys who's prejudiced against women drivers?" she asked, one eyebrow lifted with undisguised challenge.

His gaze snapped to hers and he saw the twinkle there. He grinned, his blood warming to her fire. "What if I am?"

"Then we've got more problems than whose truck to take," she said.

"How so?"

"My last name is Stevens. I'm in charge. And you're going to have to deal with me."

"I don't have a problem with that."

"You're sure?" she asked, as if there was something he should know.

"I'm positive."

It was the Lord's honest truth. As much as he wished otherwise, he was looking forward to dealing with her—more than he'd anticipated anything for a long time.

"Good," she said, nodding. "Then let me point out that I know this ranch like the back of my hand. If I drive, you'll be able to see more."

"Okay. Your point is well-taken. And there's nothing I'd like more than being chauffeured by a pretty lady."

"So WHAT DO YOU think?" Taylor asked Mitch.

"What do I think?" he mused.

She had parked her truck beside the barn and they walked the short distance to the corrals. They stood side by side with their forearms resting on the top of the fence. Well, he was standing in the dirt and she was on the first slat, but their shoulders were even— and the occasional brushing together generated a sizzle of awareness. Actually, more like sparks, which created a serious fire hazard in her parched heart. What would it take to fan the embers into flames?

Taylor tried her darnedest not to notice the subtle scent of his aftershave or the warmth of his body beside hers. She tried hard to shove the sensations to the back of her mind. She had more important things to worry about. Like getting the contract for the championships. Like *forgetting* that he was not the angry man who had told her she kissed like a little girl. Now he was very much a man. And she was a woman, standing close enough for her to feel the unbridled effects of his masculinity.

Her breath caught when his gaze met hers. She'd seen the Pacific Ocean on a cloudless, blue-sky day. She'd marveled at the breathtaking water that glittered like diamonds, yet wondered what dangers lurked below its surface. Even in the shadow of his hat, Mitch's eyes glinted, too, and she couldn't help questioning what was going on in his mind.

"Tell me what you think," she said again.

"The ranch looks good," he said carefully. "Even better than I remember. You've made some changes. Are you ready to tell me about the project you're working on?"

No, she wanted to say. She was afraid to let him know how much she needed him. It was bad enough when all she'd had to worry about was his memory of what she'd done ten years ago. But now she knew *how* he'd found out that the girl he loved had loved someone else. She knew better than anyone how deep that hurt could go.

If he'd waited for revenge, time had supplied him with the perfect means. All he had to do was hold the rodeo somewhere else. Her plan wouldn't necessarily fail, but it would take a lot longer to succeed. Time was her enemy. The added boost of publicity right out of the chute would give her a leg up on a win.

Maybe she could sidestep his question. "What are you looking for in a rodeo site?" she asked.

He thumbed his black hat higher on his forehead. "Lots of land, first off," he said.

"There has to be room for vehicle parking, and that includes horse trailers and campers. You're not too far off Interstate 20, so that's a plus."

"What else?"

"Space for portable grandstands and food vendors, a freestanding corral big enough for the events."

"I've got that," she said, pointing to the areas encircled by pipe fencing. "Three arenas, and one is long enough for the barrel-racing, goat-tying and pole-bending events."

"I noticed. What I want to know is why."

"Why what?" she asked.

"Why you have three. What do you need them for and why is the dirt soft and churned up?" He met her gaze again and asked, "What have you got up your sleeve?"

"You make it sound like I'm trying to pull a fast one."

"I didn't mean to." He turned away from the corral and leaned back against the fence, folding his arms over a pretty impressive chest.

To distract herself from his masculine pose, Taylor took the brunt of his full-on stare. Then she stepped off the fence and stood up straight. "I'm getting ready to open the ranch to visitors."

"You don't mean a dude ranch," he said, looking as shocked as when he'd gone backward into the pool.

She nodded. "B and B, Texas-style. The arenas are for activities—riding, roping. If a greenhorn takes a tumble, soft dirt is more forgiving."

"Why?"

"Because it's softer and—"

He shook his head. "I meant why are you altering the operation from a working ranch?"

"It will still be a working ranch. As long as there's breath in my body, I'll do that kind of work. But I think that will add to the charm. This is something I've always wanted to do— take people with harried lifestyles and show them what silence is like. Give them a taste of a traditional Western lifestyle."

"And?"

She didn't pretend to misunderstand. Anyone in Destiny could tell him if he asked. "I needed to do something not so closely tied to agriculture. Drought, beef and feed prices, all that can make a financial difference."

"Why is that so important now?"

"I've got a mortgage."

"Since when?" He frowned. "I thought your dad owned the land outright. Did something happen?"

"He died. Mom put the ranch up for sale."

"Why would she do that?"

"Why does that surprise you?" she asked, studying the expression on his face.

"Your family is proud. A pillar of the community. Landowners in Destiny for several generations. It just wouldn't occur to me that a Stevens would sell out." A frown settled in his eyes, making his expression dark.

Was he thinking about her sister? Jensen had sold him out with another guy. At least, Mitch believed she had, even though her sister had followed her heart.

She sighed. "My mother was born and raised in North Dallas, a sophisticated city girl through and through. She was happy here as long as my dad was alive and running the operation."

"But not after he was gone?"

She shook her head. "She missed him. And there were too many memories here. He inherited the land, so she had no emotional connection except through him."

"But to sell it out from under you," he said. "That seems a little harsh."

"Even for a Stevens," she finished for him.

"You said it. I didn't," he answered with a shrug.

"Not that it matters, but she was a Stevens

by marriage." So much for water under the bridge and not holding a grudge. It would be best not to count on any help from him, she decided. "Mom needed the money for retirement in Dallas," Taylor explained. "She couldn't stay here and didn't have the resources to get away. It was her only choice."

"And you couldn't let the land out of the family." It wasn't a question.

Vaguely she wondered how he'd known her so well. "I guess I'm like my dad in that way. It means something to me that there's been a Stevens on this ranch as far back as anyone can remember. Roots that deep are hard to pull."

"I've done pretty well without roots." His mouth hardened into a tight, straight line.

"I'm not rubbing your nose in it, Mitch. I'm just explaining why I'm in charge now."

"Okay. But why a dude ranch?"

"I'm excited about the prospect of having guests and showing them a way of life that I love. And—" She stopped, wondering if she dared expose even a hint of weakness. But she had little to lose in telling him. "I think I can make this place profitable."

"What happens if you don't?"

That was something she'd tried not to think about. All her energy had gone into positive planning. She kept telling herself failure was not an option. Now she was almost ready to open the chute and she was scared to the bone.

"Taylor?"

"If it doesn't work, I could lose the ranch," she said quietly. "Mom and Jen would help, but I want to do this on my own."

"I'm guessing that by holding the championships here you'll get publicity and word-of-mouth endorsements."

"That's right. If the right folks have a positive experience, the PR would be invaluable. Not to mention—"

She stopped. She was already lucky he hadn't laughed her from here to Fort Worth. There was no way he would actually help her unless it served his needs at the same time.

"What?"

"Nothing," she said. She turned away and started back toward the house.

Mitch fell into step beside her. "Tell me."

"First you tell me whether or not you're going to give me the go-ahead to have the event here."

They walked in silence for several moments. He stuck his fingertips in the pockets of his jeans. The memory came to her like a lightning bolt illuminating a pitch-black sky. He always frowned and stuck his hands into his pockets when he was deep in thought. Why did she have to remember that? She didn't want to recall anything about him or what had happened in the past.

It was a cruel and twisted cosmic joke that she found herself and her future dependent on the man who had no love lost for her family, and every reason to stand back and watch her fall flat on her face. She wasn't the one who had hurt him but she had a feeling that wouldn't matter. She suspected Mitch didn't have a lot of experience with forgiveness. But it had been ten years. Everyone changed. Even a mixed-up kid nicknamed Riffraff Rafferty.

"Mitch?"

He glanced at her. "I haven't made up my mind yet. There's still another site I have to check out."

"At least tell me if you think the Circle S will work."

"If you tell me what you were going to say."

Were they destined to deal with each other by dangling carrots when they wanted information? Was that any way to run a rodeo? She wished she could tell him to just let her know when he made his decision. But she had too much riding on it to walk away now.

"I was going to say that an endorsement from a famous champion bull rider would go a long way toward getting the word out." She raised one eyebrow. "That someone like you could inspire national attention—even from non-rodeo people."

"Free publicity?" he asked, but there was a grin turning up the corners of his lips.

An answering smile made her own mouth twitch. "A girl's gotta do what a girl's gotta do. I didn't major in ranch management at A&M for nothing. How can you go wrong with something free?"

They were approaching the pool and Jacuzzi she'd invested in. It made good sense that guests would want to relax and cool off after a hot, dusty ride. Her goal was to lure customers with the ranch experience while at the same time giving them all the comforts of home. Unfortunately the sight of the pool made her distinctly uncomfortable. Would it tickle his memory of that night ten years ago at the Lamplighter Motel?

If she'd been thinking, she would have parked on the other side of the house. But she hadn't had a single coherent thought since opening the door to devil-may-care Mitch Rafferty. She just hoped there wasn't hell to pay.

Please don't let him notice the pool. Or if he does, give him temporary amnesia or selective memory loss.

As they got closer, she insinuated herself between him and the pool area. If only she were taller and could block his view. Not a chance of that. He could easily see over her head.

She pointed in the opposite direction. "Look at those clouds. Do you think we're in for a storm?"

He turned to see what she meant, then glanced back down at her. "No. Those are just wispy nothin' clouds."

As they continued walking, she held out her hand to show him something else. "I plan to plant flowers over there," she said, hoping to distract him. Just a little bit farther and she would be home free. "To spruce up the place and give it color."

He looked at her. "Okay."

"And over there," she said, directing his gaze to an empty spot beside the house, "I'm considering a vegetable garden."

"In your copious free time?"

"Why not?"

"Since when did you become a farmer?" he asked, one eyebrow lifting.

"I'll do whatever it takes, be whatever I

have to be to make this work. If I can help it, no one outside the family will get their hands on my land."

"Your determination is commendable." He stopped beside the pool and looked down into the crystal clear water. When he met her gaze again, there was a flicker of something in his eyes. "But even if I choose another site, your ideas are still sound. You shouldn't have any trouble pulling in tourists."

"Not fast enough."

"What do you mean?" He asked the question but he glanced over his shoulder at the water. When he looked back, the expression in his bad-boy blue eyes sent a shiver down her spine.

She touched his arm to draw his attention back to her. Unfortunately the warmth of his strong forearm heated the skin of her palm and got *her* attention in a big way. She pulled her hand back as if she'd been burned. In a way, she had.

"If it doesn't happen this year, then next would work. Or the one after that," he said.

She shook her head. "I've got a year. After that, my capital is gone. The ranch has to be paying for itself by then. I have a limited publicity budget and this would be the best way to let people know about my operation."

"I see." He glanced over his shoulder at the water again, then back to her. "I don't remember the pool being here."

She wanted to tell him to forget about it but she held back. She had a sneaking suspicion he'd just remembered everything. "It's new. Are you leaning toward giving me the contract?"

"The Circle S meets all the criteria." The corners of his mouth turned up. "But I wouldn't want to plunge into anything. Before I have all the facts."

She swallowed hard. "Facts are good."

"Especially *all* the facts so you don't do something you'll regret. Not that I learned that from you."

Without warning, he scooped her into his arms as easily as if she were a rag doll, and held her over the pool.

Chapter Three

Mitch knew Taylor had been acting funny. Eventually he realized it was because she wasn't sure whether or not he remembered her pushing him into the motel pool ten years ago. Two could play that game. He bent his knees and lowered his arms in a sudden movement, as if he was going to drop her. She let out a high-pitched squeak and hung on to him.

He liked the way she threw her arms around his neck. But he especially liked the way she felt, pressed up against him, all sweet and feminine—with curves in all the right places, including the soft mounds molded to his chest. Her breasts. Those were definitely new, at least to him. The last time he'd seen her, when she'd plastered herself to his front and kissed him, she'd been as flat as a panhandle prairie.

Not anymore.

He swallowed hard, locking his gaze onto her face, taking in her big, beautiful brown eyes. And her mouth—so close, so kissable. All he had to do was lean forward just a bit and steal a taste. What the hell was he thinking? The answer was easy. He wasn't. At least, not with his brain.

"Let me ask you something," he finally said. He couldn't resist keeping her in suspense a little longer.

"What?" She glanced at the water below her before meeting his gaze again. "You've got me over a barrel, so to speak. Ask away."

"If you'd known I found your sister and Zach together that night, would you still have pushed me into the pool?"

"Yes," she said without hesitation, "because you deserved it. You were so mean to me, you made a hornet look cuddly."

He laughed, but it died quickly as memories washed over him—recollections of the one time in his life he was almost happy. His first love. Jen was the girl every guy wanted, and he'd thought she was his. Until the night he'd found her and Zach together. Mitch hadn't known about them, and finding them like that had sent him over the edge.

He'd lost it. Punched the guy until Jen managed to pull him off. After which she'd angrily told him she never wanted to see him again. They took off and he'd gone to brood by the pool, betrayed, angry and wanting someone else to hurt the way he was hurting. That was how Taylor had found him. She'd told him she loved him and innocently kissed him. And he'd lashed out at the one person who had given him nothing but friendship.

Only a long time later did he regret it and the fact that he hadn't had a chance to tell Jen the truth about Zach before she married him. After he'd died there was no point.

He met Taylor's gaze. "You're right. I wasn't fit company that night. But as I recall, I tried to warn you off."

"We were friends. By definition, friends try to help when there's a problem, even if it gets ugly. I don't run out on the people I care about."

"Did you care about me?"

"Yes."

She shrugged and the movement reminded him that her breasts were pressed against him. Her shapely thighs and trim waist nestled to his belly. Her soft, sweet breath fanned his face. The triple whammy sent what felt like all the blood in his body to points south. The acute awareness made him think of things he had no right to, especially about Taylor.

Thinking was one thing; acting on it would be just plain stupid.

"Speaking of problems," she said, tightening her hold around his neck, "would you mind putting me down?"

Mitch decided he would mind very much. Besides, no one had ever accused him of being too smart. When he looked into her eyes, he saw apprehension that he was sure had nothing to do with a dunking in the pool. What was she worried about? And why did it bother him that she was?

"I haven't decided where I'm going to put you," he said honestly.

She tightened her hold. "Have you changed your mind about seeing or talking to anyone named Stevens?"

"What?" He had no idea what she meant.

"That night, when I pushed you in the pool. You flat out said you wanted nothing to do with Jen or me because—"

"Your last name is Stevens," he finished.

He'd forgotten about that. Taylor hadn't. Obviously he'd hurt her a lot. She'd said she loved him, but she was only fourteen at the time. Had he been her first crush? He knew how long it had taken him to get over his first love. No doubt Taylor was over her first, too. Because a woman like her would have guys trailing after her like coyotes after a lost calf. But the idea wasn't as comforting as it should have been.

"To answer your question," he said, "I don't mind being friends with anyone. Pure friendship is a beautiful thing."

"Pure?" she asked.

"Yeah, you know. When a person likes you for yourself and not what you can do for them."

Jen had been his first lesson. She'd wanted him because her father disapproved. On the rodeo circuit, women came on to him because he was earning the big bucks and that made him famous. He'd finally learned that they pretended to care about him because they wanted their ten minutes of fame by association and what that could net.

For Taylor, it was a thumbs-up on her ranch for the rodeo site and the subsequent publicity to kick off her dude ranch. The only thing that made her different from the others was that she was up-front about it. But he would be a fool to let any appeal she might have amount to a hill of beans. No one had ever cared about him for himself. Why should he believe that she was different?

"I know how the real world works." He set her down. "I'm not a green kid anymore."

"Neither am I," she said, backing away. She pulled in a big breath and let it out.

"Do you have any idea how heavy soaking-wet jeans are?" he asked. "And boots full of water? I could have drowned."

"You deserved it. And more," she said. "After what you said to me. There were kids around the pool. They laughed when—"

"What?" he prompted.

"Nothing."

"Doesn't matter. I managed on my own." He always had and always would.

"I knew that before I walked away." She let out a long breath. "So I guess I don't have to wonder anymore whether or not you remember that pool moment," she said, trying to smile. "The question is, do you really believe it's water under the bridge as you so eloquently put it? Or are you going to hold it against me?"

He would like to hold himself against her. She'd felt good in his arms, and in spite of his self-warning, he missed her warmth and softness and the way she'd clasped her arms around his neck. But if he told her as much, he'd best wait until the pool wasn't so close. If history repeated itself, she wouldn't hesitate to push him in. He grinned, realizing in addition to her other charms, he especially liked her flash and fire.

"You mean am I going to hold it against you by turning down your request to hold the rodeo on your ranch?"

"Don't play dumb, Mitch. Of course that's what I mean. I need a big event. I need the publicity, and it has to be within my budget to make this place pay."

"Got it," he said, trying to ignore the way her earnestness brought a flush to her cheeks as if a man had just made love to her.

"And this is your chance, Mitch."

"What?" he asked, pulling back from that sensual vision. "What are you talking about?"

"You can get even with both Stevens sisters in one fell swoop." She stuck her hands into the pockets of her khakis. "In fact, this is the perfect way to get back at my father, too, for the way he treated you."

"He's gone, Taylor. Why would I want to do that?"

She shrugged. "I just wanted to put it out there. It crossed my mind. I think we should put all our cards on the table."

"But only now that you know I remember."

Her mouth turned up slightly. "Yeah. I'm a lot of things. But no one ever accused me of being stupid. If that unfortunate incident by the pool had slipped your mind, it wouldn't be very bright to remind you, now, would it?"

"I suppose not," he agreed.

"So what's your plan? Revenge or a single benevolent act to show that we've buried the hatchet?"

Hands on hips, Mitch stood by the pool, thinking. Her father was gone; he hadn't the will to speak ill of him. He had no feelings for Jen, so no wish to get even. But Taylor had never done anything to hurt him. He'd deserved that cooling off in the pool ten years ago. And he found the idea of doing anything that would harm her bothered him—a lot. She would be the one most affected by his decision.

With an effort, he pushed the thoughts away. No way was he going soft.

"I'm here to find a rodeo site. That's all. Your ranch meets the criteria. But I have one more place to check out. Grady O'Connor's spread."

"But he's the sheriff. I didn't know he was interested."

"Acting sheriff. He said he would agree to hold the event there. If necessary." He hooked his thumbs in his pockets. "If the Circle S is the best, you'll get the nod. If not—" He let the words hang between them.

"Fair and square?"

"Above reproach."

"All I ask is an honest and objective evaluation as compared to the other choices."

"That's what I'll give you," he answered. "Because this event is important for the kids."

She nodded. Then the corners of her mouth curved up and she smiled. "You're sure there's nothing I can do that might tip the scales in my favor?"

Uh-oh. Danger ahead. Her words were innocent teasing. He knew that, although he wasn't sure how. She wasn't being deliberately seductive, but damn it all, she was sexy as hell. He shot her a skeptical look, struggling for nonchalance even as his breathing quickened a notch at some ideas that popped into his mind. Top of the list: hot, slow kisses and tangled, scented sheets.

"What did you have in mind?" he asked, his voice going deeper than normal.

"They say the way to a man's heart—or in this case, his approval—is through his stomach. I could cook you dinner."

"Oh." Did he sound as disappointed as he felt?

He shouldn't even be thinking that way. For one thing, Taylor was nothing like the groupies on the rodeo circuit who had come on to him for their own agenda. For another, she was a member of Destiny's founding family. And he was Riffraff Rafferty. He always would be. That wasn't bitterness talking, just fact. Time and experience had shown him why he and Jen hadn't worked out. Because he wouldn't work with any woman. Certainly not her little sister. No matter how much he was attracted to Taylor's curvy shape, big brown eyes and hair he wanted to bury his hands in, he wasn't about to let this be anything more than business.

"I wish I could stay for dinner," he said, "but I've got an appointment. Then I've got to get a place to stay and set up a base of operations to get things rolling."

"Okay." She nodded. "Maybe another time."

"Maybe," he said.

But he would be a fool to close the distance between them. Because, as surely as death, taxes and Texas, Taylor Stevens tripped his warning signals. She was trouble—with a capital *T*.

TWO DAYS AFTER Mitch's visit, Taylor was in town at This 'n That, the shop owned by her high school friend Maggie Benson. The interior of the shop was filled with an eclectic assortment of antiques, gifts, crafts and hand-embroidered items. Maggie was an artist in her own right.

"So you're not going to tell me how it felt to see Mitch Rafferty again?" the petite redhead asked. She stood behind the high counter that held her cash register.

Taylor shook her head. "It didn't feel any way at all," she lied. "And I have to see if my truck bed is full of oats now."

"You can run, but you can't hide," Maggie said.

"My priority is making a success of the dude ranch. I want Mitch—"

"I knew it," the other woman said, her voice filled with triumph.

"You didn't let me finish, Mags. I want Mitch to pick the Circle S for the championships. Then I think I've got a shot at success."

"Then I hope he does. Because you'll buy more stuff from me, and you can send customers my way. Everyone wins."

"You're already doing a good steady business," Taylor pointed out.

"You can't be too rich or too thin."

"I'm not going to debate that with you. And first I have to get the okay from Mitch," Taylor reminded her. She glanced across the street at the tractor supply. "I need to go get my oats."

"So you can sow the wild ones?" Maggie asked, her green eyes sparkling.

"You're not funny." Taylor opened the door, making the bell above it tinkle.

"Yes, I am."

Taylor laughed and waved just before she closed the door behind her. She stood on the wooden walkway and looked up and down Main Street, Destiny. Several years ago, the town council had approved a plan to give the businesses a face-lift—a Western motif. The wooden buildings had the look of the Old West made new again. As she left Maggie's, she passed Doc Holloway's office with his name etched into the front door's oval glass. Next door was The Road Kill Café with its wooden crossbar hitching post and metal rings for looping a horse's reins.

Across from it, standing all alone, was her destination. Charlie's Tractor Supply—a sort of one-stop shopping for ranchers. She'd left her truck by the dispenser so the long hoses could fill the bed with oats, like a filling station for horse feed.

She walked across the street and Dev Hart joined her.

"Howdy, neighbor," he said. "Long time no see, little T."

"Hi, yourself," she said, smiling at the

good-looking rancher as well as the nickname he always used.

He stood beside her and folded his arms across his chest as they watched the white bed of the truck disappear beneath the oats. Dev was at least six foot two and had the sexiest indentation in his chin. His brown eyes and hair were nothing to write home about, but as a whole, he made female hearts under the age of sixty beat fast and furious.

All except hers. Because she'd learned the hard way.

Mitch had been her first lesson. Her broken engagement to Evan McCoy had been her last. The only love she would ever again permit herself would be for her land. If her heart got broken somehow, at least it wouldn't be personal. Unless Mitch had lied to her. If he wasn't fair, square and completely objective about a choice for the rodeo, then it would be very personal if her ranch went under.

It had been two days since she'd seen him, and she was about to go crazy wondering when he would make up his mind. He was worse than a kid trying to pick one thing from the candy-store case. Then she remembered that Dev was the one who had roped him into the acting commissioner's job.

Taylor moved closer and looked up at him. "Have you seen Mitch Rafferty?"

"Nope," he said, shaking his head. "But I've talked to him."

"Really?" She hoped she'd added just the right amount of indifference to the single word.

"He talked to me about the places he's already checked out for the championships, if that's what you're asking."

She smiled. "You know me too well. At the risk of presuming on our friendship, what do you think of my chances for getting the nod?"

"Good. Why? Are you worried about it?" He lifted his dark brown cowboy hat and ran a hand through his hair before replacing it.

"Considering what the Stevens sisters did to him—yeah," she said.

"That was ten years ago," Dev pointed out. "We were all young and foolish back then. Every one of us made mistakes." His words were meant to be encouraging. But there was a shadow in his eyes, and his mouth tightened into a straight line. She couldn't help wondering what else he was remembering.

"You mean Jen?"

"I mean all of us. But Jen jumped in with both feet. I'm just not sure her eyes were wide open."

"How can you say that? Was it foolish to lead with her heart? To elope with the love of her life?"

"She was only eighteen. What did she really know about Zach Adams?"

She didn't miss the fact that he hadn't actually answered her question before asking one of his own. "Jen knew she loved him and he was the only man for her. What are you saying?"

"When a girl is that young, the stars in her eyes can blind her to things. If she'd just waited, maybe—"

"What?" Taylor demanded.

He shook his head. "Doesn't matter anymore. Zach's gone."

He muttered under his breath what sounded like "Some things are best forgotten." But she knew the stubborn set of his jaw meant he wouldn't say more. Still, she wondered about the little he'd told her. She had a feeling that Mitch Rafferty's return had triggered memories for someone besides herself.

"You're in a mood today," she said. "Anything wrong? Have you heard from Corie?"

Dev had been divorced for over a year. His young wife had left him and his two-and-a-half-year-old son for a career in New York. Taylor had been engaged when she'd been jilted. She couldn't help wondering if rejection hurt more *after* the wedding.

He shook his head. "She sent a package for Ben's birthday next month with a note that said she would be too busy to see him."

Taylor touched his arm, a gesture of sympathy. "How's Ben doing?"

He smiled, but it was sad around the edges. "He's the best thing I've ever done. But if it wasn't for Polly Morgan…" He shook his head. "I don't know what I'd do without her. Full-time housekeepers and nannies don't grow on trees. And she's like a mother to the boy."

"Doesn't she have a daughter?" Taylor asked. "As I recall, she's a real brainer. Skipped a couple grades in high school."

He nodded. "Hannah. As a matter of fact, she's here now, for a visit. She's a doctor."

"Staying with you?" she asked.

"Yeah."

"Is she pretty?"

"I guess."

"Do you like her?"

"Doesn't matter. She's dedicated to her career. I need a woman like that about as much as a snake at a garden party." He shuffled his feet nervously. "Besides, I won't see her much. She's filling in for Doc Holloway while he's away on a family emergency. Started today."

"Uh-huh." Taylor couldn't help grinning. For a man of few words, that was a lot like a jump-up-and-down, kick-your-feet, put-your-fist-through-a-wall kind of protest.

"Mitch asked her to be the on-site doc for the championships—wherever they're held."

As much as she liked teasing Dev, that brought her back to her original question. Did she have a snowball's chance in hell of getting the event for her ranch?

She kicked at the dirt and gravel in the parking lot with the toe of her boot. "Jen isn't the only Stevens Mitch has a bone to pick with."

"I heard about that involuntary dip in the pool." Dev grinned with genuine amusement.

She had a feeling she was going to regret teasing him. He could give as good as he got. He hadn't even lobbed his first taunt and heat crept into her cheeks that had nothing to do with the warm May afternoon.

"Just for the record, I have no feelings for him whatsoever."

"Did I ask?" Dev said.

"It's just a matter of time," she accused. "Don't start with me."

"Look, Taylor. Ten's a lot of years. I don't

think even Mitch Rafferty can hold a grudge that long. But prepare yourself either way. Because I've also learned that the things we want the most have a way of slipping out of our rope."

Taylor wasn't so sure that Mitch wouldn't hold a grudge. The intense way he'd looked at her while holding her in his arms didn't make her believe he'd forgotten, let alone forgiven. The memory of the way her breasts had brushed against the solid, hard wall of his chest sparked heat in her belly even now. Just the way it had about every hour on the hour in the forty-eight of them since she'd last seen him. And darn it all, why couldn't she separate that conversation from the fact that he'd been holding her close while they'd talked?

With luck, she would get this—attraction, walk down memory lane, déjà vu, whatever it was—under control before she saw him again.

She glanced up the street and groaned inwardly. So much for having time to steady herself. Just then, her walk down memory lane sashayed out of the café and was headed toward her. If the thundercloud on his face was anything to go by, Mitch didn't look too happy. A bad feeling stole over her. Had he finally made up his mind? Was she going to hate the answer?

As he stepped off the wooden sidewalk, Mitch saw Taylor smile up at Dev Hart. Something inside him went white-hot with anger. What ticked him off the most was that it made no sense. Why in the world would it bother him to see the two of them together?

He and Dev had been friends ten years ago, and Mitch still didn't understand why it had worked out. But it had, and they'd kept in contact through the years. Maybe because of what happened that night at the lake a decade ago. He shook his head to clear it of the unwanted memory.

The fact was he liked and respected the other man even though Dev had had everything Mitch always wanted—family, roots and money. The roots part made him think about Taylor and what she'd said to him at the ranch. The angry feeling in his gut intensified. She and Dev had a lot in common— family and ties to the land that he would never understand. She could do a lot worse than a guy like Dev Hart. *He's not a drifter,* he thought. *Not like me.*

The knot tightened, and if he had to give it a name, he'd call it jealousy. But that was laughable. You had to care about someone to be jealous. And the ability to care had died in him a long time ago.

He stopped beside them. "Taylor. Dev," he said, holding out his hand.

"Mitch," the other man answered. A wide grin split his face as he squeezed Mitch's palm and clapped him on the back. "It's good to see you."

"You, too."

"How's it going?"

"Never better," he said.

"Oh? Problem?" Dev asked, raising one eyebrow. One corner of his mouth quirked up.

"Nope. Like I said, things are great."

"Uh-huh."

But the look on Dev's face said he didn't believe a word of it. Mitch would swear the other man thought he could see straight into his head and what he'd been thinking. But he'd be wrong. Ever since he'd returned to Destiny, memories had come flooding back. Not all of them bad. At least, not the ones about Taylor.

Like most of the guys, he'd had the hots for Jen. He thought he'd died and gone to heaven when she gave him a tumble. Only, he'd been afraid to open up with her, afraid she wouldn't like what she saw. Hell, his own mother hadn't cared enough to hang around.

Then Jen had tossed him aside for someone else, never bothering to look deeper.

But it had been different with Taylor. He'd talked to her a lot. When he'd waited for her sister, or took his practice rides on her father's bulls, Taylor was always hanging around. He hadn't thought about it a lot until now. But they had been friends until he'd angrily pushed her away.

Hell, she'd only been fourteen. And looking at her that night had been a reminder that he wasn't good enough for a Stevens. Now he was back, and she was running the ranch by herself. He admired that. He also felt as if he needed to make amends for the way he'd acted that night.

"Don't you have better things to do than stand around talking?" he asked Dev. "Haven't you got stock to tend to?"

Instead of taking offense, the other man grinned. "Sounds like you're gettin' ready to burn some powder. Since I'm not in the mood to get scorched, I think I'll mosey on over to the café. I think I see someone I know." He smiled at Taylor and touched the brim of his hat. "Nice talking with you, little T."

"You, too, Dev. Say hi to Polly for me."

"Will do. Let's get together later and catch up. See you, Mitch." Then he walked to the wooden sidewalk and stopped to talk to Hannah Morgan.

"She's changed a lot since high school," Mitch commented, looking at Hannah.

"Haven't we all." Taylor shot him an irritated look. "And aren't you just Mr. Congeniality today."

"What?" he asked.

"You chased Dev off with your charm and grace."

"I did him a favor. He was looking for an excuse to take a pretty lady to lunch," he said, glancing at the café where the two were just disappearing inside.

"Okay," she said. "Let's can the polite banter. You can give it to me straight."

"What?"

"You found a better site for the rodeo." She put her hands on jean-clad hips. She tried to hide it, but she was upset. "You chased Dev away so you could tell me in private."

He saw the slight quiver of her chin and the way she caught her bottom lip between her teeth to stop it. Her brown eyes darkened with disappointment and something that looked like fear.

"Hold on, Taylor—"

"It's all right. You said it yourself. The kids

need the best possible location to showcase their talents."

"True enough. And—"

"If the Circle S can't cut the mustard, then I wouldn't want it there."

"Me, either."

"So?" Her chin lifted slightly, and she looked him in the eye while she waited for his answer.

"In my opinion, the Circle S is the best location for the high school rodeo."

She froze, almost as if she couldn't believe it. Then a wide, bright, beautiful smile transformed her face.

She threw her arms around him. "Thank you. You won't regret this. I won't let you down."

He hugged her close for a moment, savoring the way she felt against him. As much as he was enjoying her gratitude, he had one more thing to say. He'd just figured out where he wanted to set up his base of operations. What irked him was that seeing Taylor and Dev together had done it.

"There's something else. And it could be a deal-breaker," he said, putting his hands at her waist.

"What?"

"The championships will be at your ranch. But so will I."

Chapter Four

Mitch watched Taylor's face. One thing that hadn't changed was her inability to hide what she was thinking. And right now it was a good bet she was wondering whether to say "Thank God" or "Good God." Her eyes grew wide and her full lips parted slightly in a puzzled frown.

His hands were still at her waist. She looked down at them, then met his gaze. Instantly he released her and they both backed up a step. He wished she would say something, anything to give him a clue about whether or not she was upset. She lifted her hat and tucked a strand of hair behind her ear before settling it again.

"I have to run it by the board of directors, but that's just a formality," he said.

"You mean about staying at the ranch?"

"No, holding the rodeo there. But I'll be there, too," he added.

ith her. He'd anticipated an argument and
epared rebuttals—subconsciously.

"As long as you lend your name to the pub-
city, I'll be a contented woman." She smiled
erenely.

Why did she have to say it like that, look-
ng like that? An instant picture popped into
is head. Her beside him in bed—sexy and
atisfied. Was he making a mistake moving
n with her?

All of the reasons he'd given her were
valid. He *did* have a lot to do in a very short
period of time. It would be a challenge under
the best of circumstances, but throwing Taylor into the mix added another element. They
said bull riders liked to live on the edge. That
they did it for women and money. He didn't
need either.

So why had he nodded his head in her direction?

Something about seeing her with Dev Hart,
he realized. It brought out his protective in-
stincts. She was alone on the ranch. Her fam-
ly was scattered. He'd always felt like a big
rother to her.

He ignored the voice inside trying to warn
im that she was all grown up now.

"Of course, I'll pay you for room and board,"
said.

"If the event is on my ranch, then it stands
to reason that you'll be there. Where else
would the commissioner be?"

He shook his head. "No. I mean I'm moving in beforehand to coordinate everything."

"Fine." She fiddled with the collar of her
denim shirt.

When he followed the nervous movement,
he noticed the pulse in her neck fluttering
wildly. "I think it's necessary."

"Okay."

"I have a business to run in addition to
everything involved in putting on a rodeo. I
need a space to work in that has what I need.
The Destiny motel doesn't cut it."

"I understand."

"You have a phone, I assume?"

"Yeah. I figured it was time to join the
twenty-first century, bite the bullet and put
in one of those newfangled contraptions," she
said wryly.

Her sarcasm didn't faze him. He just smiled.
"Do you have a computer and a fax?"

She grinned right back as she nodded. "The
bright young fella at the electronics store
talked me into the whole nine yards when I
got the phone."

"Well, little lady," he said, mimicking her

tone, "looks to me like you've got everything I need."

He couldn't help lowering his gaze from her face to that traitorous pounding pulse in her neck, down to her chest, waist, jean-clad legs and scuffed brown boots. By the time he looked in her eyes again, something as dangerous as a sizzling fuse attached to a stick of dynamite was churning in his gut, sending a wave of excitement coursing through him. He almost wished she would tell him her ranch was off-limits. Almost.

"Time is short, Taylor," he said, all business. "I've got a lot to do in four weeks. I need to secure equipment and supplies. Someone will have to take deliveries. Meet vendors. I'm guessing that running a working ranch in addition to finalizing plans for your dude-ranch grand opening will keep you too busy to do that."

"Okay, but—"

He rested his hands on lean hips. "Not only that, there's your whole dude-ranch thing."

"What about it?"

"You want publicity, right?"

"That's the idea," she said.

"You want an endorsement from someone well-known, shall we say?"

"Right again," she answered.

"That well-known someone can mend something he knows nothing

"Makes sense," she said.

He shifted his boots in the dirt want a genuine, no-holds-barred, come-on-down to the Circle S, I ne perience it firsthand."

"I wouldn't have it any other way.'

He shook his head. "There's a lot to do to get the rodeo up and running kids. It's a big undertaking. I can't coo that in a day or two."

"So you just said." She folded her over her chest as she gave him a patien

"Besides, you can fake hospitality couple of days. If I see for myself, I ca it a sincere thumbs-up." He took a brea know a few reporters. And I can bring influential people here for the champion If they're impressed with the B and B you'll get enough referrals to keep yo for the next two years. Minimum. I that if I stay on the ranch," he conclu if he were a lawyer presenting his ca

Her lips turned up in a small, quirk "Are you trying to convince me or yo

"You." *And myself,* he added sile

He stared at her. He'd expected no—about him being under the s

She shook her head. "A positive endorsement from former rodeo champion Mitch Rafferty will be worth a lot more than that. I wouldn't think of charging you."

He saw the stubborn set of her chin and said, "I suppose it wouldn't do any good to insist?"

"You always were quick, Mitch."

"In that case, it will be my pleasure, ma'am, to lend my name to your advertising campaign. If everything checks out."

"Fair enough." She stuck out her hand. "Welcome to the Circle S, roomie."

THE FOLLOWING DAY, Taylor watched Mitch bring a couple of leather duffel bags into her living room and set them down inside the front door. He flashed her a cocky grin and her chest tightened, her stomach dropped and her knees went weak. In her humble opinion, he made the Marlboro Man look like a wimp. If he didn't already define the word *masculine,* one glance would be worth more than a thousand words. Worn jeans molded to long, muscular legs, and the sleeves of his cotton shirt were rolled up to reveal wide, strong wrists. The sparkle in his eyes softened the lean cheeks and angular jaw but in no way diminished the effect on her female sensitivities.

What on earth had she been thinking to agree so easily to his plan? She hadn't even put up a fight—not even token resistance. And why had she felt it necessary to be here to greet him? Especially after a long, restless night of ticking off in her mind all the things that could go wrong. Starting with her apparently enduring attraction to Mitch.

But the answer came to her instantly. She was in the hospitality business now. Hospitable dude ranchers met their guests with a smile, a howdy, a "make yourself at home" and a "how can I make your stay more pleasant?" If she was going to earn his positive opinion, she would be the best there ever was at all of the above.

"I'll go out to your truck and get the rest of your things," she offered.

He aimed the megawatt gleam in his badboy baby blues directly at her. "First of all, a Texas gentleman never lets a lady carry his gear."

"But I—"

"And second, this is everything."

She rested one fist on her hip as she regarded him. "First of all, part of my service will be carrying my guests' luggage," she said, mimicking his tone. "And second, I can't believe anyone travels that light."

He shrugged. "It's the cowboy way," he said simply.

But when a dark look clouded his gaze, Taylor wondered what he was remembering that had stolen the sexy gleam from his eyes. She missed it. But all she said was "Okay. I'll show you to your room. Follow me."

He picked up the bags again, and behind her she heard the scrape of his boots on the wooden floor and his heavy step as he followed her upstairs.

"I have four bedrooms in the main house, and four cabins adjacent to the bunkhouse that are being painted," she said. At the top of the stairs, she stopped. "This open area is sort of the second-floor family room so guests can relax. There's a TV and DVD player with an assortment of movies to choose from. The furniture is new and I hope comfortable. You'll have to try it out and let me know."

"I'll do that."

"This is the master bedroom," she said, pointing to an open doorway on her left. "It's the biggest, so I plan to charge the most for it. I've added antiques and wing chairs in the sitting area. Maggie Benson made a quilt, throw pillows and the window-seat cover in material that matches the curtains."

"Maggie's still around?"

Taylor glanced at him sharply. Did he have a past with every girl in town? she wondered. Then she gave herself a mental shake. Even if he did, it was no skin off her nose. "Yeah. Maggie's got a great shop in downtown Destiny. She's doing well enough to support herself and her little girl."

"She's got a kid?"

"Nine years old now," she answered.

"I always liked Maggie," he commented.

Something pulled tight in her chest and she hoped it wasn't jealousy. "You?" She tipped her head to the side as she studied him. "I didn't think you liked anyone," she said, struggling for a light, teasing tone.

"Don't spread it around. I've got a reputation to protect."

"Right," she said wryly. "Discretion is my middle name."

He brushed past her and poked his head into the master bedroom. "This is nice."

"Thanks. Let me show you the rest." She continued down the hall and pointed to her left. "The whole back of the house has a balcony. As you can see, every room upstairs has a French door opening out onto it."

He nodded. "Impressive. I always wondered what the second floor looked like."

"You never saw it?"

"Are you kidding? Your father practically stood at the bottom of the stairway with a shotgun."

"You're exaggerating."

"Okay."

But she could tell he didn't believe her. She sighed. It made her sad that her father would never get to see how wrong he'd been about Mitch.

She opened the door to the room on her left. "This is my smallest room. But I think it's charming and comfortable. That bed is a double, so there's room for a chair and ottoman in the corner."

The bed would accommodate him, but big as he was, there wouldn't be a lot of space left over for someone else. Her cheeks burned at that unexpected thought. She had no business thinking that way. But it was hard not to while Mitch Rafferty was under her roof. That didn't bode well for her peace of mind during the next month.

She cleared her throat. "The floral wallpaper might be a bit feminine for you, but Maggie and I like it, so that's that."

She left the door open and walked to the

end of the hall. "These are the last two. They share a bathroom between them. I think it might work out well for families. Kids in one, parents in the other. They can have their privacy and be near the children at the same time." Her cheeks heated at the intimate picture she'd just painted. But she forced herself to look at him.

One corner of his mouth tilted up, confirming her suspicion that he'd noticed her blush.

"Where do you want me?" he asked.

In Kalamazoo, Michigan, she thought, but decided it would be too ungracious to say so. Besides, he couldn't help it that her hormones responded to his testosterone—in a major way.

"Why don't you take your pick?" she suggested.

He nodded. "This feels like a scene from 'Goldilocks and the Three Bears.' But I think someone's already sleeping in that bed," he said, pointing to it.

"It's mine," she confessed. "But I won't be there long. There's a bedroom and bath off the kitchen."

"Maid's quarters?"

"Originally," she said, nodding. "My folks set it up as a guest room. I plan to use it. It's comfortable and will give me some privacy from the guests while I have access to the kitchen. I didn't have a chance to move my things yesterday." She shrugged. "I didn't expect to have a customer so soon."

He walked through the connecting bath to the identical room on the other side. He put his open hand on the floral comforter and pressed down to test the queen-size mattress. Looking around, a thoughtful expression slid across his face.

He met her gaze. "This one is fine."

It had been Jensen's room before she'd left home. It was where she stayed when she visited. Taylor wondered at the knot in her chest at his choice.

"Wouldn't you be more comfortable in the master bedroom?" She leaned against the doorway and folded her arms across her chest to take her mind off the ache there. "After all, if you're going to sing my praises, you should experience the best room in the house."

He looked out the window, then turned and shrugged. "This is fine. I can see the arenas from here. And the pool," he said, raising one eyebrow. "Pools have fond memories for me," he added, a twinkle in his eyes.

"Are you sure?"

He nodded. "Seems like it will be easier on you."

"How do you figure?" she asked, wondering how she would be able to sleep with him so close.

"If we're not spread out all over the house, I'd just guess it would be more efficient. Not to mention sharing a bath. Gotta be easier than maintaining two while I'm here."

He had a point. She planned to hire some help, but until then she was responsible for upkeep. But cleaning more rooms might be worth it to put some distance between them. Surely he would be more comfortable in the master bedroom on the opposite side of the house. A room so close to hers couldn't be the appeal, although a tiny glow flickered to life somewhere in the region of her heart.

With his back to her, he stood looking out the window. "You and your sister must have had quite a time growing up in this house."

Instantly the glow sputtered out. And it was so simple she was surprised that she hadn't seen it immediately. He'd picked this particular room *because* it used to be Jensen's.

Before she could stop it, a pain zigzagged through her. Even though she knew better, she hadn't been able to prevent it. A testament to the power Mitch Rafferty still held over her. And only one small tile-and-porcelain room between them. Just what she needed.

Another challenge to getting through the next four weeks.

First priority would be to move to a separate floor and into the maid's quarters.

He turned from the window and met her gaze with a quizzical one of his own. "Earth to Taylor."

"Sorry," she said, rubbing the bridge of her nose with one finger. "I guess my mind was somewhere else. Did you say something?"

He crossed the room and stood in front of her. "I just wondered if you found it lonely here now that the rest of your family is gone."

"No. Anywhere else I probably would be, but not here on Stevens land. My roots are here and they go deep," she said. Then she noticed the flicker in his eyes. "I'm sorry, Mitch. I know that's a sore spot. I didn't mean to touch on something uncomfortable for you."

He shook his head. "It doesn't bother me. Not anymore."

"So you've come to terms with your past?"

"Part of it," he said.

The part that didn't include Jen, she guessed. But she'd already stuck her foot in her mouth once. Wild horses couldn't drag a question about her sister from her lips.

"So where do you call home now?"

He shrugged. "Nowhere. At least, I don't own property anywhere," he clarified.

"Surely you don't live in a cave?" she teased. "That'd be tough. Cave property in Texas is scarce."

He grinned. "Under a rock is more like it," he answered, joking back.

Times like this were the hardest, Taylor thought. This was when she missed him most, when he baited, bantered and bothered her.

This was when she was in the most danger of making a damn fool of herself all over again. Time to head for the hills.

"Well, that's the whole tour. I've got work to do, so I'll leave you to settle in," she said, hoping she didn't sound too abrupt. But she had to get out of there. She started backing out of the room.

He followed. "To answer your question, I lease a condo in L.A. My business is based there."

"I see," she said as they walked side by side down the hall. He would no doubt be going back when his obligations in Destiny were fulfilled. "Do you like California?"

"Yeah," he said, nodding. "But I'm looking for other opportunities around the country. There are areas of Texas growing faster than anywhere else in the country. Industrial and business centers and shopping malls are going up fast."

"Really?"

"That's right. Actually, Destiny is growing. I'm looking at some projects around here."

"So is that why you took on volunteer work for the rodeo? Business contacts? Put your name out there?" *Selfish reasons?* she wondered to herself. She probably shouldn't have asked. But when had she ever kept her mouth shut when she should have?

"The exposure doesn't hurt," he admitted. "Dev mentioned it when he put the bite on me. But it's not the only reason. I don't need to work ever again, Taylor. I made enough money riding bulls that with sound investments I could live comfortably for the rest of my life."

"Assuming you didn't squander it on wild living." She flashed him a smile, then held the railing as she started downstairs.

"Yeah, assuming that," he said with a chuckle. "Or if too many people hit me up."

"Who would do that?"

"My mother, for one."

"You heard from her?" Taylor asked, shocked. She stopped, midstairway, and looked at him.

He stopped on the step below her so she met his gaze squarely. "Yeah. You know that whole under-a-rock thing is genetic. Ruby came out from under hers and managed to track me down when she found out about all the money I was making."

"Is she still married to the construction guy?"

"*Still* would be the key word. I have no proof that they ever got hitched in the first place. But she's single now, living in Vegas. Working in a casino."

"So she wanted money," Taylor mused. "Did you give it to her?" As soon as the words were out of her mouth, she realized how invasive they were. "Scratch that. Sorry to be so nosy. You don't need to answer."

He shook his head and they continued down the stairs. "No big deal. Yeah, I gave it to her. I've learned that everyone wants something. At least she's kin."

It was a small glimpse into the most eligible cowboy's life. She remembered the magazine stories. Her head told her that was a long time ago. Her heart believed he traveled in fast-paced, exciting, glitzy circles. Places she couldn't go. But now he was telling her there was a downside to money and fame. She could see it in his eyes, and the look there tugged at her sympathy.

"Everyone wants something," she said quietly. "Including me."

He stepped off the bottom stair and turned, blocking her. Her front was touching his front and they saw eye to eye. It would be easy to rest her forearms on his shoulders, the familiar way couples did. She could touch her mouth to his with little effort and let him deepen the contact. She wanted him to fold her in his arms and hold her.

Suddenly this house she knew better than the back of her hand was the loneliest place on earth.

He shrugged. "You never get something for nothing," he said. "That's something else I learned."

"I wouldn't have it any other way. When I get your seal of approval, I'll have earned it fair and square. Or I don't want it at all."

Otherwise it would mean Mitch Rafferty was just being nice to her. Or worse— feeling sorry for her. And that meant she would have to watch her back as far as her heart was concerned.

A sweet and considerate Mitch Rafferty was more dangerous than a no-limit card game with the devil.

Chapter Five

The morning after a restless night, his first in Taylor's house, Mitch stepped out of the shower. He knew she'd been there not long before. Her scent lingered, giving him an instant visual of her naked—soft skin, lush curves, sleek and wet and— Whoa. Annoyed at the train of thought he couldn't tame, he grabbed his shaving kit and unzipped it. After pulling out razor, toothbrush, toothpaste and comb, he looked for a spot to put them on the vanity. A good portion of the space held Taylor's toiletries.

Body lotion, body splash, body mist. *Body.* The word jumped out at him from every single, solitary product in the whole damn bathroom.

His annoyance kicked up a notch. What had he been thinking to pick the only room in the place where he had to share such inti-

letter word. Ranch work keeps me busy and active. It's better than one of those designer fitness facilities and a lot more fun."

"And very effective." As soon as the words were out, he wanted them back like a no-point ride. But it was almost impossible to look at her curves and not want to explore every last one.

Holding a spatula, she glanced at him over her shoulder and grinned. "Did you just pay me a compliment?"

"Nope."

"I didn't think so." She turned back to what she was doing, pouring this and that into a pot and whipping it up.

Mitch looked around the kitchen and out the glass door to the patio with a slatted covering over it and the pool beyond. It brought back memories of that night ten years ago when she'd kissed him and said she loved him. He couldn't help wondering how she about him now. More specifically, what would happen if he kissed a grown-up, filled-Taylor Stevens?

Trouble, that was what. And he'd had enough lifetime. Starting with his mother walking out. Taylor was a class act. Now that she wasn't a kid, he doubted she'd be interested

mate space with Taylor? Only her bedroom would be worse.

Or better.

Jeez. He couldn't seem to stop. He hadn't had a sensible thought since the day he'd come to the ranch to check it out. The day he'd seen Taylor Stevens again—all grown up.

He grabbed a towel and dried his hair, then wrapped the thick, luxurious terry cloth around his waist. After brushing his teeth and hair, he dressed quickly in his room. There was a lot to do in a short amount of time to get the show on the road. He needed to get his mind off Taylor and things he had no right thinking about. But he needed caffeine first to do both.

When he opened his door, the aroma of fresh-brewed coffee drifted to him, as if the B and B fairy had read his mind. That smell along with the aroma of freshly baked biscuits, sweet rolls and bacon made a hole in his gut as wide as the Texas prairie. Even stronger than his hunger was an urgency to see Taylor. And for the life of him he didn't understand why, let alone have the will to control it.

He peeked through the open door into her room and wasn't surprised to see that her bed was neatly made. Following where his nose led, he found his way along the upstairs hall and down to the kitchen.

Taylor stood at the stove, her back to him as he walked in the room. Her sun-streaked brown hair was arranged in a French braid with the ends tucked up, leaving her neck bare and him with a yearning to kiss that sweet-looking spot. The hem of her pink cotton blouse disappeared into the waistband of jeans with the seat so worn, it was practically white, almost transparent. He flexed his fingers, aching to see if she was as soft, supple and shapely as she looked.

When his gaze lowered again, he noticed that she wasn't wearing her boots. White socks covered her feet and he found himself wondering what they would look like bare. Did she paint her toenails?

Enough, he thought, really irritated with himself. Coffee, breakfast and a long day of work in that order were what he needed to get his mind back on business and off one pretty lady rancher.

"Morning," he said.

She glanced over her shoulder and smiled. "Good morning. Did you sleep well?"

"Great." It wasn't a complete lie.

He'd slept like a rock when he'd finally fallen sleep. He couldn't fault the room or

the bed for the amount of time he'd tosse turned. But the B and B proprietress w other story. Thoughts of Taylor had kep awake for a long time.

"Coffee?" she asked.

"I'd be in your debt forever," he answ fervently.

She poured him a cup and brought where he stood outside her U-shaped area. She put cream, sugar and arti sweetener on the counter, then a spoor stirring.

"Are you hungry?" she asked.

His gaze automatically went to her Definitely hungry. But not for food.

He forced the thought from his mind he said out loud. "I think I could eat

"Sorry. That's not on the Circl You're going to have to settle for e biscuits and gravy, home-frie sweet rolls, fruit and juice."

"Jeez, a guy could starve arc

"I know," she teased back. comes of just having girls arc Everyone but my father was time or another."

"Really?"

"No," she said, lifting a stove to check the conter

in a guy like him. No matter how much time had passed.

Mouthwatering smells made his stomach growl and he could hardly wait to eat. He sipped his coffee and a feeling of contentment slipped over him. There was only one other time in his life when he'd felt anything even close.

It was that small window of time when he'd thought Jen had been his. But there was more and he couldn't quite grasp the memories lurking in the shadows. Jen was the girl of every guy's dreams. He'd always had to be on his toes when they were together. Then he got it, as if the "aha" light went on in his brain. Talking to Taylor had been different, relaxing. He'd always felt better after their conversations. Little sister was safe. If she laughed at him, what did he care? She was just a kid.

At that moment, she turned to the side and lifted her arms, reaching up into the cupboard. Her cotton blouse pulled tightly across her breasts, clearly outlining the full softness. He gripped his coffee cup so tight his knuckles turned white, then he swallowed against the dry tightness in his throat.

Little sister was a big girl now. No way was she safe. If he had half the brains God gave a gnat, he would remember that. Because she'd been his friend then, and seeing her again had made him realize that he'd missed that friendship. He didn't want to jeopardize it.

And crossing over the line to some man/woman attraction complication could jeopardize the good thing they had going again. He'd messed it up once; he didn't make the same mistake twice.

"We're ready to eat," she said.

"Good. I'm about to keel over." And not from hunger.

"You go sit in the dining room," she instructed.

"What can I do to help? I can carry something in."

She shook her head. "You're my guinea pig. I plan to treat you like a paying customer, so you have to act like one."

"But, Taylor—"

"I insist," she said, passing him with a covered casserole in her hands. She disappeared into the dining room, but her voice drifted back.

"I need your endorsement, but I don't want what I haven't earned. And it has to be honest and fair. Besides, now is the time to work the bugs out, before I have guests." She returned to the kitchen and looked up at him. "You're my first."

I wish.

The thought popped into his head before he could stop it. Of course she'd meant her first guest. But he'd gone straight to boyfriend. Main squeeze. *Lover.*

Her first? Had there been someone else for her? Of course. What was he thinking? She was a knockout. Guys probably lined up for miles. Dev Hart for instance. The two of them had everything in common. And neither would have to walk down Main Street Destiny with a bag over their head. But the thought rankled. It tore through him, leaving a path of anger in its wake.

"Please sit down. I'm tired of walking around you. And you're too big not to get underfoot."

Her tone reeked of teasing, the way she might treat a big brother. Everything in him rebelled at the thought. She brushed by him again on another trip from the kitchen. This time she carried a cloth-covered basket with out-of-this-world aromas coming from it.

But it wasn't enough to cancel out her subtle, sexy scent. She smelled like a Texas prairie filled with spring wildflowers. He couldn't help remembering all those lotion bottles in the bathroom with the word *body* on them. *His* body suddenly went hot and hard.

Seemed a good time to do what the bossy lady had said. He walked into the dining room and sat, then reached for the napkin and put it in his lap. "Do you plan to order the paying customers around like that?" he asked.

She set steaming dishes of potatoes and eggs laced with onion, green pepper and pimento on the table. "My current plan is to be a gracious hostess and treat my guests as I would like to be treated. But yes, I would tell them as diplomatically as possible that if they want to eat, it happens faster if they don't fence in the cook. This is a home as well as a business and I want them to experience my way of life."

He took the bowl of scrambled eggs she held out. "It's nice. Your way of life is a good one."

Her gaze never left his face and questions swirled in her eyes. "Why are you like a tumbleweed in the Texas wind?"

He grinned. "The way you say it makes me sound like a legend in my own time. Or the pitiful subject of a country-and-western song."

"I didn't mean to," she said, her mouth turning up at the corners. "But I'm serious.

Why didn't you ever put down roots, Mitch? Was it because of what happened with Jen?"

"I can't deny that probably didn't help. But I got a booster, in case I forgot."

"What do you mean?"

"I was engaged once, while I was still on the circuit."

She held a spoonful of potatoes in midair, a shocked expression on her face. "I didn't know."

"You mean there was something that didn't make the tabloids?"

"I can't say. Only that I never heard."

"Just as well. The rest of the sordid details were in every magazine and gossip column."

"What happened?"

"It turned out that she was sleeping with the All-Around Cowboy."

"Makes you wonder which three events he scored highest in," she commented.

"*Rodeo* events," he clarified. When Taylor's cheeks pinkened slightly, he knew she got his drift. "But Barbara Kiley, the girl I came this close to making the little woman, gave *All-Around Cowboy* a whole new meaning."

"I'm sorry."

He shrugged. "It was after I hurt my leg

and decided to give up the rodeo," he finished.

"Oh, Mitch—"

"It's okay. My name was in the record books. I got promotional gigs. But she wanted to be in the spotlight. To be on the arm of the guy currently getting the publicity. I wasn't that guy anymore."

"I'm sorry," she said again. "I don't know what else to say."

"It was a long time ago. Besides, that wasn't the first time I came in number two. It's no big deal."

Memories of that initial year on the rodeo circuit washed over him. Watching Jen and Zach together. Knowing what the guy had done, the mess he'd left behind in Destiny. Knowing Zach wasn't good enough for Jen and not being able to say anything. She wouldn't have believed him.

So he'd tried to ignore them. Tried to forget the ache in his gut. He'd done his best to concentrate on his sport and beat Zach Adams in every event where they squared off. Success was the best revenge. And Mitch won overall money. But he never got to be number one— not till Zach was killed. Now he would never know if he was better.

"Wandering isn't a solution, Mitch. There

isn't anywhere on earth safe from emotional baggage."

"You're right. So I've chosen not to participate. I'd rather channel my energy into other things. Like business."

"I know what you mean. You're not the only one who's had a broken heart twice."

"Twice?" he asked.

She nodded. "I was engaged, too. About eighteen months ago."

He was unprepared for the instant and powerful assault of jealousy. The question on the tip of his tongue was whether or not she wanted him to make the guy sorry for treating her that way. But what he asked was, "You said twice. There was someone else?"

Her gaze lowered and she pushed her eggs around her plate with her fork. "That's not important."

"What does that mean?"

"Just never you mind."

"Did you catch your fiancé cheating on you?"

"Not exactly." She sighed and put her fork down, then wiped the corners of her mouth with her napkin. "When we met, he told me right up front that he was getting over someone else."

"Give the guy a brownie point," he said sarcastically.

"He never lied to me, Mitch. He was honest and straightforward. So when he said he loved me and wanted to marry me, I believed him."

"What happened?"

"His old girlfriend decided she wanted him back."

"And he went?"

She nodded. "He said he hadn't stopped caring about her and it wouldn't be fair to me." The sunny look she'd worn since he'd first seen her this morning disappeared.

"Low-life jerk," he said.

Mitch wanted the guy responsible for hurting her to pay. Five minutes alone, no questions asked. He wanted to take him apart. Wasn't that what an honorary big brother did? That was the part he was here to play. He let out a long breath. It was a tough assignment and more involved than he'd realized. A reminder that her father had been right—he wasn't good enough. A big clue that a guy like him, who didn't know the first thing about being part of a family, was wrong for her. And the worst part—he knew his anger, not to mention the thoughts he'd had since waking up, weren't in the least brotherly.

"It hurt at the time, but I'm over him now," she said a little too brightly.

"You don't have to pretend with me."

"I'm not. I don't say anything I don't mean." She picked at a half-eaten biscuit. "Destiny is still a good place to settle," she said quietly, then met his gaze.

"Maybe from where you're sitting. It never felt all that good to me."

But he looked at her. She was sitting at a right angle to him, close enough that he could reach out and cover her hand with his. He found he liked talking to her. He must. He didn't just blurt out the unfortunate fact of his engagement to just anyone. What would it be like to share breakfast with her every morning? To come home at night to a woman like Taylor? Have her kiss him hello and talk about his day with her and listen while she told the events of hers. And children.

Whoa. There must be something in the air or water in Destiny. He wasn't given to flights of fancy like this. At least, not in a long time. Not about hearth, home, having someone. He wasn't the solid, steady, stable type. He *was* like a tumbleweed and he came by it naturally. It was in his genes, and biology was tough to overcome.

He continued to eat in silence, putting away

a fair amount of the food she'd cooked. Finally he put his fork down. "I'm stuffed. That was great. The best meal I've had in a long time."

"Really?"

"You're not the only one who says what you mean, Taylor. I can't remember when I've tasted better."

"Good," she said, smiling shyly at his compliment.

"Now I need to get to work." He stood up.

"My office is in the front of the house. You're welcome to use it," she offered. "That's where technology central is located. I expect you'll need the squawk box and all the rest of the electronic gizmos."

She smiled, but it didn't quite work and he wondered why.

He nodded. "Thanks. If you don't see the whites of my eyes by suppertime, take a peek to see if I'm still breathing."

"No problem."

LATER THAT DAY, Taylor was still in the funk that had started when Mitch had told her about his engagement. She couldn't shake the black mood and she'd finally figured out why.

"I feel more alive than I have in ten years

and it's all because of him," she muttered to herself.

She jammed the pitchfork into the hay, then brushed her forearm across her sweaty brow. She remembered Mitch talking about being number two. "He feels like number one to me," she said to herself, letting out a long breath.

"He's been burned twice. Surely he won't want to try again. To go for number three, he'd have to be as dumb as a wagonload of rocks. They say third time's the charm, but he's not the trusting sort."

Did she even want to be his number three?

She'd been burned twice, too, and he'd been the first. She kicked at the hay with the toe of her boot. "I'd have to be an idiot."

"Who's an idiot?"

She whirled around and saw a man silhouetted in the barn doorway. If the deep, sexy voice wasn't enough of a clue, she would know those broad shoulders, narrow hips and long legs anywhere. "Mitch, you startled me."

"And you're scaring me. Standing here talking to yourself." He walked the length of the barn and stood just outside the stall where she was working.

"Occupational hazard," she mumbled, her heart pounding. The devil of it was, the hammering wasn't because he'd surprised her. It was just that he was there dressed in jeans, with his long-sleeved shirt rolled to just below his elbows.

She took a deep breath. "I don't often have anyone else around to talk to. And as far as I'm concerned, it's always an intelligent conversation."

Unless, of course, she was wasting her own time, talking to herself about Mitch Rafferty.

"Speaking of occupational hazards, I saw some of the bulls you're keeping for Dev."

"How? Did they crash the computer room to access the internet?"

He grinned. "I was looking for you. Ran into Jim Foster down in the pasture. He told me you were up here."

"Did Jim remember you?"

He nodded. "I can't believe he's still here. He was foreman ten years ago."

"He worked for my dad as far back as I can remember. He's like family. I don't know what I'd do without him. In fact, now he sees to most of the day-to-day running of the ranch. Did you meet Cal White?"

The teenager she'd hired reminded her of Mitch. He had the same intensity and ambition to succeed. One big difference was that he had supportive parents.

"Nice kid," he said, nodding. "The two of them were checking out the bulls."

"So what does that have to do with me and occupational hazards?"

He leaned one broad shoulder against the stall doorway. "I'm glad it wasn't you working with animals big enough to crush you like a dried leaf." The teasing note disappeared from his voice. He looked dead serious.

Was he worried? About her? The first thought that popped into her head was that she didn't know what to do with what he'd just said. Her second, she wasn't thinking at all, simply feeling a lovely, warm glow in the pit of her stomach. Followed quickly by annoyance when his comment sank in. He was treating her like a little girl.

"I'm not a kid anymore," she snapped. "Believe it or not, I've done ten years' worth of growing up while you've been gone."

"I can see that."

"Get used to it. I'm a grown woman, Mitch."

"I know," he answered, mumbling something that sounded like, "believe me."

"I know what I'm doing. Dad taught me everything he knew, and Jim took over where he left off. I wish you'd start taking me seriously—"

"Down, girl. At ease," he said, holding his palms out in surrender. "I get the point."

"I'm not so sure. You're acting like my big brother. And I don't need one. I can take care of myself."

"Are you trying to convince me or yourself?" he asked.

"You." She walked out of the stall with the pitchfork in her hand.

He nodded at the sharp prongs. "Do you plan to use that on me?"

"If I have to." But she couldn't prevent it when her mouth turned up at the corners. She'd run out of steam and couldn't resist his teasing. Lord knew she wished she could.

"So why aren't you taking care of the bulls?"

"Jim's showing Cal what to do and he said I was in the way."

"There seems to be a lot of that around here," he said wryly, referring to what she'd said while putting breakfast on the table. "And the general impression is that Texas is a big place. Who knew people could get underfoot on an annoyingly regular basis?"

"I needed to do some work here in the barn," she added.

"Don't you have cheap labor for this?"

She nodded. "But they don't start till tomorrow. I'm saving the rest for the hired help from the high school rodeo team. But they're finishing up school finals." She rested the pitchfork prongs on the ground and leaned on the handle. "I plan to give the kids lots to do when I fill the guest rooms. They can work with any greenhorn who wants to learn about horses, or ride, or rope."

"Is that so?"

"You bet. The teenagers have a lot of knowledge to share. My clients will benefit and just think how good the kids will feel about themselves. I figure my busiest months will be summer when they're out of school so there should be a steady supply of labor."

"What will you be doing?"

"I'm the brains of the outfit."

"Chief cook and bottle washer?"

"Pretty much," she confirmed. "I'll make sure everything runs smoothly at the house. Organize activities—hayrides, campfires, trail excursions. If we have a group of children, I figure I'll handle showing them around. Maybe I'll set up a petting corral where they can touch the animals and feed them."

"Everything from creekside cookouts to cozy campfires," he said.

"That about covers it. And I'll have to re-

member those words for the advertising bro-
chure I'm putting together." She closed the
stall gate and started out of the barn, stopping
in the toolroom to replace the pitchfork. Her
breath caught when she came out and saw
that Mitch had waited for her, then fell into
step beside her.

"You've thought of everything," he commented.

Not quite. She'd never thought about what
it would feel like to see him again, let alone
to have him under her roof.

That morning she'd awakened with a sense
of anticipation she hadn't experienced in a
long time. She'd had to keep reminding herself that she was practicing on Mitch. But she
couldn't quite get her heart to buy the balo-
ney. She'd been as happy as a cat in a cream-
ery. Right up until he'd told her about his
engagement. It was like a dousing with ice-
cold water and twice as bracing. He'd been
in love with someone else.

*Do not make the mistake of falling for
Mitch Rafferty again,* she warned herself. Her
father's words came back to her: *One mistake
is acceptable. The same mistake is just plain
stupid.* She'd been a girl the first time, but
she was a woman now. And the pain could
be so much worse.

"Is there some reason you were looking for me?" she asked.

"I called a reporter friend of mine to set up a time for an interview. Publicity for the championships. She's going to bring a photographer along."

"When?"

"Day after tomorrow."

They walked out of the barn and Taylor stopped for a moment, letting her eyes adjust to the sunlight.

"That will work," she said, nodding. "So when the reporter's here, she can tie the rodeo and my operation into the article."

"Right."

Suddenly the full impact of his words sank in. "You're giving me the endorsement? So soon?" she asked. "You've only been here a day, and you're ready to sing my praises publicly?"

"Breakfast was really good," he said with a grin.

She shot him a skeptical look. "You're not just feeling sorry for me? I don't want that—"

He shook his head. "I like what I see, Taylor. No kidding. And I think a lot of folks will, too. I meant it when I said yours is a good way of life. I consider it a civil service to give you a recommendation."

Taylor believed him. Maybe it was just because she wanted to so badly, but she did.

She threw herself into his arms. "I can't believe it! A thumbs-up from the legendary Mitch Rafferty, bull rider extraordinaire." She kissed his lean cheek. "Thank you. Thank you. Thank you."

"You're welcome," he said, a smile in his voice.

Closing her eyes for a moment, she savored the contact. It was risky, especially when he fell into that sweet-and-considerate category she was so leery of. But she couldn't help it.

Then she felt him tighten his grip, snuggling her more securely against him. Cold-feet time.

"What will the neighbors say?" She wriggled out of his arms, a second after meeting his amused gaze.

"Probably nothing since the closest one is a left turn past yonder."

"Yeah." She backed away and stuck her fingertips into her pockets. "Anyway, I'm really grateful."

"Glad to help," he said simply.

In silence they started walking again. As they neared the pool area, she noticed that his limp was more pronounced than she'd seen before. "Are you okay?"

He nodded. "Just stiff. And part of the reason I came looking for you to tell you about the reporter. I needed a walk to work the kinks out of it."

She slipped off her boots so as not to track muck over the decking. Walking past the pool, she stopped just outside the sliding door that led into the kitchen eating area and set her boots beside the patio mat.

She glanced back at Mitch where he stood staring into the crystal clear pool water. Something about his expression tugged at her heart. In her stockinged feet, she walked back and stopped beside him.

She met his gaze. "That must have been a difficult time—the injury and everything. It must have been tough to make the decision to leave the pro circuit."

"Considering the alternative, that part was easy. Surgery, pins, screws and plates in my leg was hard. Not to mention rehabilitation afterward."

"Still, you were young. I hope what's her name at least hung around until you got out of the hospital."

"I don't remember."

The dark intensity in his eyes told her differently. "I know you'd never admit to it in a million years, but you were probably scared."

"You're right."

"You were scared?"

He shook his head. "I'd never admit to that in a million years."

"You don't always have to be the strong, silent type, you know."

"I'm not being any type. But I do believe that what doesn't kill you makes you stronger."

Taylor bent over to dip her hand in the water. "Nice." She stood. "Not too cold. And the Jacuzzi might help the stiffness in your leg—"

Suddenly he scooped her into his arms, as easily as if she were a five-pound sack of potatoes.

"What are you doing?"

"I also believe in don't get mad, get even."

She shook her head. "Haven't we been through this before? You didn't throw me in then, and I don't believe you'll do it now. All talk and no action, Rafferty."

"If you yank a rattler's tail, you best brace yourself for the bite." There was a devilish grin on his face as he walked to the deep end of the pool.

"You wouldn't dare," she warned him.

"I never could resist a dare."

The next thing she knew, she hit the water fanny first.

Chapter Six

Mitch watched for Taylor to surface. He wasn't quite sure why he'd thrown her in, except maybe to wash away the sadness in her eyes on account of his leg. Since he was a boy, folks had looked at him with the same expression she just had, because he was the kid no one wanted. But he was luckier than a whole lot of people and he didn't need anyone's pity.

Ever since he'd returned to Destiny, he'd had a nagging sense of putting away the past, making peace with it. On top of that, another feeling pestered him: that she worked too hard and needed some fun in her life. He figured a mad-as-hell Taylor was better than the serious woman he'd just ambushed.

"You son of a rabid coyote," she shouted. "Why did you do that?"

He shrugged as he stared down at her. "You looked hot."

"I wasn't, but I am now," she shot back,

pushing wet hair out of her eyes. She stroked through the water and reached the side of the pool, where she hung on. "These jeans are heavy."

"I seem to remember something about that." He reached a hand down to her. "Unlike you, I'll help you out."

"Because you're a nice guy." She only hesitated a moment before grabbing on with both hands. "A true Texas gentleman," she said wryly. There was a gleam in her eyes and saccharine dripped from the words. "How's your leg?"

"Fine," he said, but her tone had warned him.

He was prepared when she braced her feet against the side of the pool, then yanked for all she was worth. He could have resisted easily, but he let her pull him in.

He surfaced almost instantly and saw her struggling to climb out. "No, you don't."

He reached out with one arm and seized her around the waist, hauling her up against him. He settled her back to his front.

She tried unsuccessfully to break his grip. "Let me go. We're even now, Mitch."

"Nope. You're still one up."

"But you're a Texas gentleman," she reminded him.

"I've been living in California. The West Coasters weirded it out of me," he answered.

Looking over her shoulder, he was distracted by the sight of her breasts, just above where his arm encircled her waist. Her pink cotton blouse, so crisp and clean just that morning, was now wet and all but transparent. Her white bra was clearly visible beneath the soaked material. He could practically identify the brand, and it wasn't satin or lace. Just serviceable cotton, plain and practical. He swore he could see the dusky shadow of her nipples. Water everywhere, but his mouth went dry.

Heat flashed through him in spite of the cool water. It didn't make any difference that a perfectly respectable tank suit would show more skin than she revealed in her drenched clothes. But Taylor Stevens wet and in his arms made him think about things he shouldn't—about how she would look *without* the layers of clothing.

He didn't know he'd loosened his grip until she suddenly turned in his arms and lunged halfway out of the water to get the leverage she needed to push on his shoulders and dunk him.

When he surfaced, she was trying to get away, stroking for the shallow end of the pool. "Not so fast," he said, reaching after her. "Cheaters never prosper."

"I didn't cheat. All's fair in love and war." She glanced over her shoulder and squealed when he stretched out his arm and caught her slender ankle. Slowly he pulled her toward him. "This is war," she said, trying to pull her foot away.

"Damn right it is." He could stand on the bottom, giving him the advantage he needed. Gripping her waist, he lifted her and arced her body up and into the water with a splash.

She came up laughing and shrieked as he made a move toward where she was treading water. "You've got me on size and strength, Rafferty. But I'm not above using teeth and nails as weapons."

"A true Texas lady," he said, grinning.

"A girl's gotta do what a girl's gotta do."

"Okay. I give up," he said. He held up his hands.

She blinked and pushed her dripping hair out of her eyes. "Wow. If you'd been in command at the Alamo, Texas would still be part of Mexico."

"I don't want to hurt you."

Her brown eyes flashed fire. "Don't you worry your pretty little head about that. I'm tough."

He couldn't take his eyes off her mouth and remembered a night ten years before when she hadn't been so tough. Since then, very few things had surprised him as much as what Taylor had done that night. She'd said she loved him, then kissed him—an innocent touch of her mouth to his. After leaving town, he'd put Destiny—and Taylor Stevens—out of his mind.

Coming home again resurrected all the memories. Now the only thing that amazed him more than Taylor's sweet kiss was that he could still see the hurt in her eyes, the way her mouth had trembled. Just that morning, she'd confessed her busted engagement. He'd seen a familiar expression on her face, pain and betrayal mixed together. He didn't ever want to be responsible for hurting her again.

He swam to the side of the pool, his will to spar sputtering out. But she wasn't giving up. She followed and tried to dunk him, putting all her weight into pushing on his shoulders. He braced himself and she couldn't budge him.

"There's more than one way to skin a cat." She cupped her palms just at water level and pushed a wave into his face.

Tossing his head to scatter the drops, he grinned. "Now you've done it."

"Oh, yeah? I'm shaking in my boots."

"You're not wearing boots."

Then he started splashing, and his hands were twice as big as hers. She kept at him, though. She just wouldn't give up. Definitely a tough cookie. He couldn't help admiring her for that. But he could see she was tiring and took pity on her.

He held his hand up and put the other on top, forming a *T* for *time-out*. "You win," he said, knowing that was the only way to get her to stop.

"You give up?"

"Yeah."

"It's a trick, right?" she asked. "A ploy? Playing possum? Lull me into a false sense of security so I'll let down my guard then you go in for the kill."

"I wouldn't do that."

He hung on to the side of the pool, and she glided next to him, laughing as she grabbed hold of the coping and faced him. She rested her elbow on the edge and dragged in several gulps of air as she concentrated on catching her breath.

Mitch looked at her mouth. He might go in for the kiss. In that instant he realized his mistake. But wild horses couldn't make him look away from her full lips. Their faces were barely an inch apart. He could feel soft puffs of her breath on his cheek. Her chest rose and fell rapidly, drawing his attention to her breasts. She was no longer off-limits. At least not because of her age. He remembered the little girl she'd been. He wanted to taste the woman she'd become, see how she would feel. Would she respond to him or had he destroyed that by pushing her away ten years ago?

Before he could talk himself out of it, he brushed strands of hair off her face, then threaded his fingers through the heavy mass. He encircled the slender column of her neck with his palm and gently urged her toward him.

Surprise and something else leaped into her big brown eyes. She'd caught her breath from their tussle, but now her breathing was quick and unsteady. Again. He hoped she was winded for the same reason he was—an attraction he couldn't seem to ignore no matter how hard he tried or all the reasons he reminded himself it wouldn't work.

Before he could think it to death and stop himself, he captured her lips with his own.

Her mouth was cool, wet with droplets of pool water. More than that, she was soft and sweet. With his fingers threaded through her hair, he gently urged her forward to make the touch of their mouths more firm. She tipped her head sideways to deepen the contact.

His heart hammered in his chest. Liquid heat sluiced through him driven by the blood that raced through his veins, fueling his desire. He traced the seam of her lips with his tongue and instantly she opened to him. Dipping inside, he stroked the honeyed recesses of her mouth.

Just when he'd thought it was safe to go back in the water, he was in danger of going up in flames. Their wet shirts were practically nonexistent, and he could feel the heat of her skin when she pressed her softness to his hardness. Her honestly eager response delighted him. His will to hold back was just a microthread from snapping.

Taylor was consumed with desire at the first oh-so-tender touch of Mitch's fingers brushing the hair from her face. Why did he have to be sweet? She was powerless to resist that. She expected him to turn his back, ignore her, push her away. If he'd just followed his usual pattern and kept his distance, she'd have been okay. But the soft and gentle feel of his big hands in her hair was her undoing. All her self-warnings became ashes in the wind.

Her skin felt hot and her heart pounded

madly. He was so strong, so masculine, so sexy. And so achingly romantic. The feel of his mouth, the touch of his long, strong fingers, the wall of his chest against the softness of her breasts. It was every bit as wonderful as she'd dreamed. And she prayed he would never stop, but the prayer wasn't working for her.

Almost the next instant, he pulled back. His breathing was ragged and a perfect match for her own. His gaze burned into hers.

"You kiss like a woman," he said.

The little pocket of hurt she'd carried around for ten years disappeared. There wasn't anything he could say that would have touched her more. "Thank you, Mitch. That's high praise coming from Texas's most eligible cowboy."

"Not anymore," he said. He let her go and hauled himself out of the pool, buckets of water pouring from his jeans onto the decking. "I took myself out of the running."

He held a hand down to her, and she grabbed on and held tight as he easily pulled her out of the pool. Her heart squeezed painfully at the words. They were a between-the-eyes reminder that he'd been hurt badly. She knew wounded animals were likely to strike back and it wasn't smart to get too close. She already knew how painful it was when Mitch had left her behind. To go through it again would be plain stupid.

She would take his words about her kissing technique, and his kiss, in the spirit he'd no doubt meant them—a white flag to put the past to rest.

"Now I think we're even," she said, hoping her voice was light and steady.

"Yup." He ran a hand through his wet hair.

Were his fingers shaking? No. Not cool, calm, collected Mitch Rafferty. It must be her imagination. She stood in the puddle her sopping jeans had made and looked down at herself. Her blouse was practically see-through. Embarrassed, she felt the heat climb up her neck and into her cheeks. After pulling the tails of her shirt from her jeans, she tugged the material away from her chest, trying to salvage some modesty.

She wrung out the bottom of her blouse to hide the fact that her hands were shaking. "Playtime is over."

"You're right about that."

"I have a business to get off the ground. You have a rodeo to put on."

"True enough."

"We wouldn't be the brightest bulbs in the chandelier if we let ourselves get carried away."

"Can't argue with you there," he said. "We're not allowed to have too much fun."

Anytime now he could stop agreeing with her, she thought crossly. "I think I'll go inside and get some towels. The laundry room is right there," she said, pointing to the door on the left. At least she wouldn't trail water through the house.

"Thanks."

Was that all he could say after that bone-melting kiss? Suddenly angry, she wondered what women saw in the strong, silent type. The appeal was highly overrated. Give her a man in touch with his feminine side any day. Maybe a man like that would say what was on his mind and a woman would know what was going on. She could do without the guessing games, thank you very much.

"Taylor?"

"What?" She glanced at him over her shoulder.

"I'm going into Destiny this afternoon."

"I don't need to know your comings and goings."

"I probably won't be back for dinner."

"Oh." The anger slid away in the wake of her disappointment. She needed to work on feeling nothing. "Thanks for letting me know."

Without looking at him again, she walked toward the house, leaving him behind her by the pool, just like ten years ago. Unlike ten years ago, he'd initiated this kiss.

So why didn't she feel a whole lot better about it?

AFTER CLEANING UP from his unscheduled dip in the pool, Mitch drove into Destiny. He told himself important rodeo business couldn't wait. He needed to see his old friend Sheriff Grady O'Connor. But in his gut he knew this trip into town had everything to do with Taylor. More specifically, the way he'd felt after kissing her.

Right outside in front of God and everyone, he'd wanted to pull her back into his arms and pick up where they'd left off. Which would have been a big mistake. It was also his motivation for the decision to go into town. But he refused to believe he was behaving like an army in full retreat.

He parked his truck in front of the sheriff's office and went inside. The auburn-haired female deputy at the front counter greeted him. The nameplate beside her said Deputy Phoebe Johnson. Behind her were several metal desks holding computers and littered with paperwork. File cabinets lined every spare inch of wall space. Overhead, fluorescent lights glared down.

"Can I help you?" she asked.

"I'm here to see Grady O'Connor."

"Your name?"

"Mitch Rafferty."

"I'll let him know you're here," she said, picking up the phone beside her. "Mitch Rafferty to see you, Sheriff. Yes, sir, I'll send him right in."

She met his gaze and Mitch touched the brim of his hat. "Thanks," he said, pushing through the swinging door.

He walked down the hall, glancing into the open doorways of the three offices he passed until he saw a familiar face behind a gray metal desk.

"Grady," he said, walking into the room. But his friend wasn't alone. A tall, green-eyed brunette stood beside him.

"Hi, Mitch," Grady said, standing. He held out his hand. "You remember Melissa Mae Arbrook."

Mitch shook hands, then looked at the woman, trying to recall. "Melissa Mae."

"You don't remember me, do you?" she asked, her full mouth somewhere between a smile and a pout. "Arbrook is my married name, although I'm divorced now," she added pointedly. "My last name used to be Allen. At least I didn't have to change the initials on my luggage," she added with a shrug.

"It's been a long time," he said, hazy memories surfacing. He'd had a short fling with her in high school—before Jensen. "How are you?"

"Fine. I work at the Road Kill Café."

Something about the juxtaposition of those two comments made Mitch smile. "How's it going, Grady?"

"Can't complain." The sheriff was tall, about the same six-foot-two-inch height as himself. But his brown hair was cut military short. Blue eyes filled with amusement gazed back at him.

"Well, he should—complain, that is," Melissa Mae said. "I brought him a sandwich because he always misses lunch. Between sheriffing, running that big ranch of his and being daddy to the most adorable nine-year-old twin girls, the poor man runs himself ragged."

"Sounds like you could use some help," Mitch commented. It was obvious Melissa Mae Arbrook was trying out for the job.

"I'm doing just fine," Grady said.

"How about you?" Melissa Mae asked, moving in close to Mitch.

Apparently she wasn't especially choosy about who she auditioned for. The scent of her perfume was strong from across the room. Up close, the fumes made him want to cough. "I can't complain."

"Is there a Mrs. Rafferty?"

He shook his head. When her green eyes gleamed with interest, he kicked himself for being so quick to tell the truth.

"Y'all must be lonely, then," she commented. "In spite of the fact that you're staying with Taylor Stevens."

"How did you know?"

She shrugged, drawing attention to her generous breasts beneath the logo on her white T-shirt. "It's a small town."

The phone rang and Grady answered it instantly. "Sheriff O'Connor," he snapped out. He listened for a moment then said, "I'll tell her." He looked at Melissa Mae as he set down the receiver. "Bonnie says to quit flirting with anything in pants and get your fanny back to the café pronto."

"I swear she's a female Attila the Hun," Melissa Mae grumbled. "I would leave her high and dry if I didn't need the job so bad—" She took Mitch's arm and smiled up at him provocatively. "I'm finished with my shift at eight."

"Is that so?" He knew what was coming.

"Let's get together. I want to hear about everything you've been up to for the last ten years. Then maybe we can pick up where we left off in high school."

The memory of kissing Taylor flashed through Mitch's mind. Talk about picking up where you'd left off—the sensual haze from the sparks they'd created just that afternoon closed around him again.

"My last ten years haven't been all that interesting up until today," he said.

Thinking he meant her, she smiled. "All that could change tonight," she answered. "I've been told I can be pretty entertaining."

He was debating whether to take her up on her offer when a pair of laughing brown eyes and full, smiling lips popped into his head.

"I have other plans." Shuffling his feet, he glanced at the woman holding on to him. "But thanks for the invitation."

"All work and no play—" she said, leaving the thought hanging. "I gotta go, but you think it over. If you change your mind, you know where I'll be. Bye, Grady. Mitch," she said, then sashayed out the door.

Grady cleared his throat. "You'd have to be deaf, dumb and blind to miss the fact that she wouldn't throw your boots out the front door," he commented wryly.

"I didn't miss it," he said. "I'm just—"

Not interested? Since when did he turn down a pretty woman with curves that made a man's mouth water? A vision of Taylor flashed into his mind—soaking wet and spitting mad. Then the image changed and he remembered sparkling eyes full of humor and fun. Not to mention her determined chin with the intriguing indentation that had beckoned to him more than once to explore. And last, but by no means least, her sexy little body with lush curves and soft skin.

If he hadn't kissed her. And held her in his arms. And talked to her... Maybe then he could have taken Melissa Mae up on her offer. Since his broken engagement, he'd perfected the technique for an uncomplicated relationship. His fling from a decade ago would be easy to walk away from. He'd already done it once. A voice in his head said he'd done the same to Taylor, but that didn't change the fact that he had trouble getting her out of his mind now.

"Mitch?"

"Hmm? What?" he said, meeting Grady's gaze.

"Something tells me that woolgathering

you're doing has nothing to do with Melissa Mae Arbrook and everything to do with a rancher whose name is Taylor Stevens."

"Define 'something.'"

"That 'until today' remark." Grady leaned back in his chair and rested his linked fingers over his abdomen.

He glared at his friend. "I hope you work at law enforcement with more than guesswork, because you're reaching in the dark on that one."

"I don't think so. One simple fact can take a skilled sleuth from point A to point B with a small margin of error." Grady shrugged.

"What simple fact?"

"You've got the hots for Taylor."

"That's a pretty big leap."

"Not really. It's a fact that you're staying at her place. Like Melissa Mae said, it's all over Destiny."

"You gotta love small towns."

"And last I heard, there aren't too many women on the Circle S. Jen works in Dallas. By process of elimination, Taylor is there."

"What makes you so sure I've got the hots for her?" Mitch demanded.

"You didn't deny it."

The sheriff was right—about everything. He just didn't know about the kiss. But Mitch would rather lose the biggest development deal of his life than share that information or admit straight-out that he *did* have the hots for Taylor.

And it was even more clear after seeing Melissa Mae again. Something had changed for him. No way did he want to start a fling with her or anyone else, for that matter. Including Taylor—especially her. But he couldn't get her off his mind. She'd said she loved him once. Granted she was a kid at the time, but he wondered how she felt about him now.

Mitch let out a long breath as he looked at his friend. "Grady, it's my professional opinion that you've been cooped up behind that desk too long."

"Professional what?" Grady asked in a tone that said he didn't believe it for an instant.

"That's a good question," Mitch admitted. "You know Dev strong-armed me into putting on the championships."

The sheriff nodded. "What can I do for you?" he asked.

Business. Good. Something to take his mind off Taylor.

"I need to talk to you about providing security for the championships," Mitch said.

"You didn't have to come all the way into

town for that. Why didn't you pick up the phone?"

No way would he admit to the real reason. "I figured we could mix business with a chance to talk about old times."

"I wish I could. But now's not a good time. After I wolf down this sandwich, I've got a meeting with the mayor."

"How about tomorrow?" Mitch asked.

He looked at his desk calendar and shook his head. "Nope. The girls have a checkup. They're excited about it for the first time ever. And believe me, when they're not in favor of something, rounding the two of them up takes patience, skill and all the sweet-talking I can manage."

"So what's different? The new sawbones in town?"

"Lady physician," he clarified. "But I guess you know about her taking over for Doc Holloway."

"Yeah. I met her. Dev was helpful in convincing her to fill in at the rodeo."

"So I guess my girls aren't the only ones happy she's in town for a visit." Grady was still looking at his calendar. "How about the day after tomorrow? I'll come out to the ranch."

Mitch nodded. "I have a meeting with a

newspaper reporter in the afternoon, but that shouldn't be a problem. I'd like Dev to be there, too, check out the facilities and see if there's anything he needs."

"Sounds good. Like old times. All of us together."

"Except for Jack," Mitch said.

Grady frowned. "So you haven't heard anything from him, either?"

"Nope. But I moved around a lot at first. It would have been hard for him to track me down."

"From what little I heard, finding you would hardly work up a sweat for Jack Riley. Rumor had it he was tagged for some elite military group after he joined the army."

"So he's never been back to Destiny?" Mitch asked.

"Once. Briefly. When his dad died. It would be good for the four of us to reminisce about old times." The words were right, but there was a shadow in his eyes. He hadn't forgotten that night by the lake, either.

"So we're on for day after tomorrow."

"I'll see you then." Grady took a big bite of his sandwich. His mouth was full, but Mitch still made out the words "Say hi to Taylor for me."

"Okay."

Mitch left the office and got into his truck. Since he'd told Taylor he wouldn't be there for dinner, would she read anything into the fact that he was back so soon?

He read enough into it for the both of them.

Chapter Seven

Taylor stepped into the bathtub for what would probably be her last upstairs soak. It was a good opportunity. Mitch was in Destiny and had said he wouldn't be back for dinner. Tomorrow she planned to move her things to her permanent room off the kitchen.

After rolling up a towel and placing it on the porcelain rim behind her head, she relaxed and closed her eyes, enjoying the scented mountain of bubbles surrounding her. At first when Mitch had said he wouldn't be there for dinner, she'd been disappointed. And she'd found his absence left a void, making her angry. He'd been there less than twenty-four hours. How could there be a hole in her life? But now, as she experienced her tension easing in the warm water, she couldn't help feeling that when life gave you lemons, you made lemonade.

Right now, Mitch Rafferty was her lemon.

If only he hadn't come back. If only he hadn't kissed her. Damn the man. What had he been thinking?

A shiver rippled through her as she remembered the feel of his lips against her own. If her bathwater hadn't already been warm, the heat from her skin would have taken the chill off. Why had she responded to his touch? She wasn't a kid anymore. She was a grown woman and she wasn't carrying a torch for Mitch Rafferty. She wasn't. Truly.

She could just hear Jen: *If you have to work that hard to talk yourself out of it, there must be an element of truth.*

Taylor shook her head as she gathered the bubbles close to her body and propped her feet on the side of the tub. If only she could figure out how to make lemonade from her attraction to Mitch.

"Nope. I won't care for him again. He's leaving after the championships. I won't let him make a fool of me a second time."

"Are you talking to yourself again?"

That was Mitch! His voice was coming from the hall. She hadn't closed either door to the Jack-and-Jill bathroom. There was no way to make lemonade out of this lemon. But what she wouldn't give for the world's biggest towel.

"You're not supposed to be here," she squeaked.

"It's a good thing I am," he continued, his voice getting closer. "If you keep talking to yourself, people are going to start wondering about you. The loony lady who lives by herself on the big ranch. That kind of reputation could do a number on your business." He poked his head around the corner.

"Get your mangy carcass out of here," Taylor squealed, sliding down below the bubble line. The hand towel behind her went, too, and was now soaked. "There are laws against this sort of thing in Texas."

"Sorry. I didn't know you were taking a bath." But his wide grin said otherwise.

"You said you wouldn't be here." She had nothing to cover herself with. Her tiny loofah was about as useful as two wagons in a one-horse town.

"I changed my mind."

"Why? Nothing exciting going on in Destiny on Saturday night?"

"I wouldn't say that. Melissa Mae Arbrook let me know she's available."

Taylor snorted. "No kidding. Available is her middle name. Ever since her divorce." What was she thinking having a conversation while she was stark naked except for some

If the shoe fits," he said.

"So who hit you with the poetry stick?" e asked, failing utterly at extinguishing the ow his words produced. Instead the warmth read from her belly and radiated outward, aveling at lightning speed to every part of er.

"Why is it so hard to believe that you are 1 attractive woman?" He opened a cupboard nd closed it again when he saw it contained lates.

"They're in the hutch in the dining room," ne said, turning to go get something to put ne wine in.

She opened the glass door and retrieved two ong-stemmed crystal glasses, then joined him 1 the kitchen, keeping the bar between them. le poured the chardonnay into each one.

He met her gaze. "You didn't answer my uestion. Why don't you believe you're at- active?"

She didn't have any wish to deny it. "My ster was a tough act to follow. It's pretty ard to compete with perfection. And after y engagement went bust, I figured it was ne to get real, to stop trying." She shrugged. 'm just me and that's just the way it is."

He handed her one of the glasses. "You're ot a quitter."

flimsy covering that she could hear popping even as she spoke? "Get out of here, Mitch."

"Why? It's not like I have X-ray vision to see through those damn bubbles. Besides, after that dip in the pool, I saw more through your blouse."

She threw her loofah at him, but it missed and hit the wall when he ducked into the other room, laughing.

"You're not a Texas gentleman and it's a lie if you say you are! You're a black-hearted, transplanted-to-L.A. Texan who doesn't have the chivalry of a rattlesnake."

"I'm a guy who wouldn't be human if he didn't do his best to get a peek at a pretty lady."

He thought she was pretty? Taylor grinned, although she would rather eat glass than let him know his sweet-talking had worked. "The least you could do is go downstairs so I can salvage my modesty and get out of the tub."

"Go ahead. I won't look."

"Like I believe that."

"Scout's honor, Taylor."

"When were you a Boy Scout?"

"I have the heart and soul of one," he said, but there was humor in his voice.

Her mouth curved up in spite of herself. "You're incorrigible."

"Some things never change."

"This water is getting cold enough to freeze the horns off a steer. I'm going to have to trust you. But if I catch you looking, just remember I have a pool and I know how to use it."

"Words to put the fear of God in a man," he said, a truce in his voice. "I'm afraid to tangle with you. I'll meet you in the kitchen."

Taylor listened carefully, and his heavy steps grew faint as he went downstairs. Quickly she got out of the tub and grabbed a bath sheet, pulling it around her. She let the water out, then went into her room and shut the door. After drying off, she pulled on undergarments then a peach-colored pair of knit shorts and a matching top. She brushed her straight hair into a ponytail on top of her head, letting wayward strands around her face fall wherever. Some blush and a little lipstick were the finishing touches.

When she left her room, there was a glow in her heart and a spring in her step. All because Mitch Rafferty was downstairs. There was a big void in her world when he wasn't around, but he was a big man. Flutters in her stomach kicked up like the Rockettes at

Radio City Music Hall. Damn it, what was good for her, she woul diculous reaction to Mitch under tween here and facing him in her

But when she padded barefoot int the hitch in her chest at the sight o her no such luck. He was turning a in a wine bottle, his back to her. Wh traordinary sight. In his white shirt, long sleeves rolled to his elbows, he s standard for masculinity. His broad sl tapered to a narrow waist where his disappeared into his jeans. Lean hips a legs completed the picture that unsett susceptible heart. She should turn awa and go back up to her room. But she For two reasons. She was no coward. A still needed his approval for her dude-promotion. Both good reasons.

"So, Mr. Peeping Tom," she said.

He glanced over his shoulder and gr "Lighten up, Taylor. I didn't see squ sides, you're always wearing work shi jeans. When do you get a chance to sh those beautiful shoulders? And that pink toenail polish?"

"Next thing I know you'll be telling teeth are like stars, they come out a and my eyes are like—"

"I don't believe that's quitting," she shot back. "But for argument's sake, how would you know?"

"I just do. The girl I remember from that night ten years ago didn't give up on a jerk who lashed out and tried to push her away."

"As I recall, I was the one doing the pushing." She took a sip from her glass and let the smooth, cold liquid slide down her throat.

He grinned. "That's what I mean. You don't take any guff."

"Look, Mitch, I don't want to talk about me."

"I do."

Taylor watched him take a drink. A lot of guys would look like a sissy holding a delicate crystal glass instead of a longneck bottle of beer. But Mitch Rafferty had more masculinity in his pinky than most guys. He oozed macho and was so darn good-looking her heart hammered painfully in her chest.

"What about me?" she asked, hoping she wouldn't regret the question.

"You said you loved me that night."

She wished he hadn't said that at the same time she was taking a drink. The wine went down the wrong way and she started to cough at the burning. Mitch was around the counter in three strides and patting her on the back.

"You okay?" he asked, holding her by her shoulders.

"Fine," she said, eyes watering. "Look, Mitch, there's nothing I'd rather do than forget about that night."

"Me, too. But I can't. I was hoping we could get it out in the open, discuss it, then put it away for good. Did you mean what you said?"

"I was fourteen years old. Of course I meant it." She took a deep breath. "But you were right."

"I like that. About what?"

"I was just a kid. A skinny one at that."

"You were right, too."

"That's always good," she said, flashing him a grin. "About what?"

"You said I should wait and you would show me."

"I was angry. I didn't mean—"

He settled his knuckle under her chin and raised it, forcing her to meet his gaze. "You're beautiful. When you walk down Main Street Destiny, I bet you give guys whiplash."

"You're exaggerating. I don't—"

"You're a woman now, Taylor. You're not a skinny little girl." He shook his head in wonder and admiration. "Lady, you showed me big-time."

Suddenly all her self-warnings were about as substantial as dust in the Texas wind. He was so charming, so sensual, so—everything.

Her heart skipped when he cupped her jaw in his palm. The intense expression in his bad-boy blue eyes shot a shiver of desire straight into her feminine core. When he slipped a strong arm around her waist and snuggled her against the solidness that was him, she turned into a quivering mass of jelly, and his lips hadn't even touched hers yet. Her bare legs brushed against his denim-clad ones, creating a friction that spread through her like wildfire, threatening to make her go up in flames.

Then he lowered his head and his lips met hers. The soft contact stole the breath from her lungs as he slowly and thoroughly explored her mouth. Then he branched out, kissing her closed eyelids, her nose, her cheek, her jaw. He nibbled his sexy, seductive way down her neck and stopped at a spot just behind her ear. Tingles exploded over her shoulders and arms and stole over the rest of her body. *He* stole her will to resist. But she had to find the strength to pull away. She didn't want to hurt again the way only Mitch could make her hurt.

That rational thought was like a high-beam headlight through a fog bank. It gave her the split second of clarity and resolve that she needed. She took his face between her hands and tenderly kissed his cheek before slipping out of his arms. Instantly, achingly, she missed the exhilarating feeling that only being close to Mitch gave her.

"I don't know about you, big guy, but I haven't had dinner yet," she managed to say on a shaky breath.

"Can we talk about this?"

When he reached out a hand and tucked a strand of hair behind her ear, Taylor was almost lost again. Not counting the one ten years before, that was kiss number two. She didn't want to go for three. She didn't believe in "third time's the charm." Kiss of death? It would be better not to find out.

She took a step away from him and tried to smile. "I don't think there's anything to say. Let's just forget this ever happened."

He drew in a breath. "Okay."

She hadn't known how much she wanted him to disagree with her until he didn't. But it was for the best. Truly.

And her sister, the lawyer, would have a

field day telling her anyone who protested that much was probably as guilty as sin.

TWO DAYS LATER, Taylor was still struggling to get that kiss out of her mind. Although the visit from Mitch's reporter friend helped. Now they were outside snapping pictures for the article while the woman directed as if she were a Hollywood heavy hitter.

"If I were you, Taylor, I'd hire Mitch, Dev and Grady just to hang out on the ranch. Business will boom. Women will flock to the Circle S. Guaranteed."

Taylor glanced at Grady, Dev and Mitch— the testosterone trio beside her. There would be no living with them. Mitch's reporter friend had done it now. Ann Crandall had arrived at the ranch right about the same time Dev and Grady showed up for their meeting with Mitch about the rodeo championships.

"I could use the extra work, little T." Dev grinned at her.

Grady laughed. "I don't think I've got the time. But maybe you could do a life-size, stand-up, cardboard representation of me. For that I'd only charge you a onetime, dirt-cheap flat fee. Should bring the ladies in."

"Maybe Melissa Mae Arbrook." Mitch laughed at the other man's shudder. "Don't sweat it, guys. With me here, Taylor doesn't need you."

Texas was big, and Destiny more wide open than some places. But Taylor had a feeling there would no longer be space wide-open enough for their egos in the Lone Star state.

"You just did the local hatmaker a favor." Taylor smiled at the late-twentyish reporter Mitch had called in a favor from. "Their heads just grew several sizes, and now custom-made Stetsons are the only way to go."

"You're no slouch, either, lady," the woman said, making notes in her spiral book. "Has anyone ever told you you're a Sandra Bullock look-alike?"

Taylor blushed at the compliment. "No way. I—"

"I haven't talked to a man yet who would throw her out of his bed. Right, Walt?"

The photographer stopped snapping pictures and lowered his camera. "You got that right, Annie. Girl-next-door type works for me every time."

"See what I mean?" Ann said, looking at them and nodding with satisfaction. "When Walt gets finished with these pictures, we'll run them along with this article on the high school championships. I'll run a small side piece on the ranch, along with the fax and reservations number you gave me, in syndicated papers across the country. I think you're going to have more business than you can handle. And not just the female kind." The short, plump, gray-eyed brunette raised one eyebrow as she studied the four of them posed by the fence outside the barn.

"Definitely a good representation of the best Texas has to offer." She looked at her notes. "Now, let me make sure I've got my facts straight. Dev, you're the stock contractor who provides the animals for the rodeo. You're a bachelor raising a young son?"

"That's right," he answered.

"And Grady O'Connor. You're the town sheriff and a rancher. What was the name of your place?"

"Miller's Mound. The land was in my late wife's family."

"So you're a widower? A bachelor. Any kids?"

"I've got twin girls, nine years old," the lawman said. "Someday the ranch will be theirs."

Taylor smiled at his obvious discomfort with the attention. For all their good looks and joking, none of these guys seemed especially at ease in the limelight.

The reporter turned away and said to her

photographer, "I think I've got what I need. How about you?"

He nodded. "We have to go through downtown Destiny to get to the interstate. I'll shoot a few there."

Ann nodded. "Taylor, Mitch, guys," she said, looking at each one. "It's been a pleasure."

Mitch shook her hand. "Thanks, Annie. I owe you one."

The reporter shook her head. "That exclusive interview you gave me after your injury was the break, pardon the pun, my career needed. Now we're even."

"Okay. You take care. And thanks. You, too, Walt," he said, shaking hands with the photographer.

After the news media left, Taylor glanced at Dev, Grady and Mitch. Two out of three were grinning at her like indulgent big brothers. But Mitch looked like a tornado about to touch down.

He shuffled his boots in the dirt, then rested his hands on his hips as he stared down at her. "You know, Taylor, when her piece comes out, you could be busier than you expect."

"I'm not worried. I've got lots of help on

the ranch—Jim, the hired hands and the teen-agers will be coming and going all the time."

"Hiring the teens is a good thing," Mitch commented. "Keeps them busy and out of trouble."

"You should know," Grady said, grinning good-naturedly.

"Do you hear me arguing?" Mitch glanced at his friend then met her gaze again. "But you need to make sure you're not in over your head, as far as hired help goes."

"Are you hinting that she should hire you, Rafferty?" Grady snapped his fingers. "I know, Taylor. Mitch could be your body-guard."

She chuckled, hoping he was joking. Hoping more that they wouldn't pick up on the fact that her smile was phony-baloney. The mere idea of Mitch guarding her body sent shivers of anticipation coursing through her.

"What makes you think he's not already doing the job?" Dev said.

Mitch glared at the two of them. "Don't you guys take anything seriously? Especially you, Grady. You're the law in these parts."

"I have a sense of humor," the sheriff said, shaking his head. "And I know how to use it. A good cop knows when to be serious and when to lighten up."

"Seems sensible," Taylor said.

Mitch glared at them. "Why don't you two wait for me at the house? If you think your swelled heads will fit through the door."

"Okay." Grady lifted his hat and settled it more firmly on his head.

"Can we help ourselves to the sweet tea?" Dev asked.

Taylor nodded. "What kind of hostess would I be if I didn't let you make yourselves at home?"

The two men sauntered in the direction of the house and she was alone with Mitch.

"Taylor, I'm serious. It never occurred to me until Annie started talking about guests. Are you really prepared?"

"I think so, but I won't know until the chute opens, will I?" she asked, speaking in language she knew he would understand.

"I don't know—"

"Don't worry." She put her hand on his arm, and the warmth of his skin seeped through her palm, then raced through her body, heating her everywhere. "I'll be fine. I've given it a lot of thought, planning and preparation. This is something I've wanted to do for a long time. I'm looking forward to meeting people. It's business, but also a social outlet I think I've needed."

"By social, do you mean men?" Intensity jumped into his blue eyes.

Taylor backed up a step. "What if I do?"

"Do I have to tell you you're playing with fire?"

"I know how to play. I survived you, didn't I?"

"Never mind me. The point is that—"

"The point is nothing." She tucked a strand of hair behind her ear that the wind blew across her face. "You're not my bodyguard. You're not my big brother. We have no connection and you have no responsibility toward me at all."

And none of her words washed away her wish that it was different.

"Taylor, listen to me—"

She shook her head. "You're leaving, Mitch. When the championships are finished, you're out of here. Why should I listen to you? I appreciate the fact that you're concerned about me. Really I do. But after you're gone, what difference does it make? You'll do whatever it is you do and I'll take care of my life, my ranch. My roots."

"Just because I'm not here doesn't mean I won't care about you. And worry about you."

"It's not necessary." She shrugged and hoped it was casual, that he couldn't hear her heart thumping in her chest. But she couldn't help smiling. "If you'd been this nice ten years ago, Destiny would have had to put out a help-wanted sign for a new local bad boy."

He stared at her for several moments, then started to laugh. He shook his head. "You're a pistol, Taylor Stevens."

"Takes one to know one, Mitch Rafferty."

"You never really knew me, Taylor," he said. He started to walk toward the house.

"Mitch?" She waited until he stopped, then glanced at her over his shoulder. "I knew you then. I know you now. You're not riffraff. You're a nice man, a *good* man, and it's about time you stopped trying to hide the fact."

"A vicious lie and I will deny it to anyone who asks."

The sight of his broad back built a sigh up inside her, but she managed to hold it back until there was no way he could hear.

"I am in so much trouble," she said to herself.

a longneck bottle of beer, his favorite
nd. Apparently she was noticing things
ut him, too. Then she grabbed an opener,
ked off the cap and handed the bottle to
1.

I have a feeling you can use that."

You're a good woman, Taylor."

he gifted him with a wide, bright smile,
something between pleasure and pain
lled in his chest. He realized these past
ks here at the Circle S were probably the
piest he'd ever known. On the circuit, he'd
peted day in and day out, half the time
even knowing what town he was in.
fter the injury, he'd channeled his energy
college classes, his degree, then getting
business off the ground. But somehow,
r seeing Taylor again and spending time
h her, he was beginning to feel ties. To
tiny? To her?

oots?

'm just whipping up some rice, chicken
fry and vegetables. Do you want some?
ade enough for two in case you came
le for dinner." She glanced at him over
shoulder.

id she realize what she'd just said? That
as home? He'd never really felt that any-
re. His life had been a series of foster par-

Chapter Eight

Mitch drove up the long ranch road, then
pulled his truck to a stop in front of Taylor's
house. He leaned his head back and drew in
a big breath. The championships were a week
away. He'd been working long hours on and
off the ranch to make sure the event happened. When he wasn't busy with that, he'd
been tied up with a development deal not far
from Destiny. The planning meeting he'd just
left had ended after eight and they were picking up again early in the morning. He was
tired to the bone and all he could think about
was seeing Taylor. Busy as he was, nothing
had kept him from thinking about her, wor-
rying about her when he wasn't around.

It had been three weeks since the reporter
had interviewed her. Three weeks since the
night he'd kissed her and she'd pulled back.
They'd shared a lot of meals since then, and
idle chitchat, but nothing more intimate. The

kiss had done something to her, and not in a good way. She'd been polite, friendly, but distant. And she'd moved her things to the room downstairs off the kitchen.

He should have been grateful. She was a woman who knew what family was all about and he was a mutt no one had wanted. They were oil and water. She would be better off with Dev Hart or Grady O'Connor. Anyone but him.

If only he could get that message from his head to his heart.

Now that she was no longer in the bedroom across from his, he found he missed her—and not just her fragrance and froufrou body stuff in the bathroom. He missed *really* talking to her. Mini conversations about the weather just weren't up to his usual standards and expectations from Miss Taylor Stevens. Suddenly he couldn't wait any longer to just see her. He opened the truck door and stepped out.

He let himself in the house and dropped his briefcase in the office at the front just off the entry. Then he went in search of Taylor.

He found her in the kitchen. Cooking.

He couldn't help grinning when her flowery fragrance drifted to him and he realized by that and her clothes she'd just bathed. He drank in the sight of her legs, bare below her

white shorts. Her formfitting [...] stopped just at her waist, but when [...] up into the cupboard, he was tr[...] sight of some smooth midriff ski[...] side, he could see that her prett[...] squeaky-clean and without makeup[...] pink scrunchy held her sun-streak[...] hair on top of her head.

If she brought up the weather, som[...] was going to turn the conversation t[...] thing personal if he had to take he[...] arms and kiss her senseless.

He cleared his throat so she woul[...] startled. "I see someone else is just [...] home from work."

She turned and smiled at him—[...] inely warm and welcoming expressio[...] beautiful brown eyes before the shutt[...] down. "Howdy, stranger."

"If that's your way of saying I'[...] busy, you're not just whistling 'D[...] have you."

"You're right. But how did you k[...]

Because he knew her routine, her [...] and the fact that when she was wo[...] wore jeans. He didn't see her bare [...] her workday was finished.

"Just a guess," he said.

She opened the refrigerator door [...]

ents, then a rented room when the department of social services had cut him loose. But this place—and Taylor—were getting under his skin. He just wasn't sure whether or not he was happy about it. Every time he'd sat on a bull, he'd been prepared for a rough ride. He didn't think there was any way to get ready for the twists, turns, ups, downs and pain of a relationship. He didn't have what it took.

Mitch took a drink of beer. "Dinner's the best offer I've had all day."

"Sounds like you haven't had a very good day. Want to talk about it?"

He shook his head because he wanted to very much. The idea was too appealing. But he didn't like what that meant. The idea of sharing himself with her made him want to hop the bus to parts unknown before he got in so deep he couldn't get out.

"So what have you been up to?" he asked, turning the conversation away from himself.

"I've been training my hired help. All of 'em are good kids and I think they'll work out great. Cal White especially. I wish I could keep him here forever. He works hard. He's fun and funny. And he takes part of his pay to ride the bulls we board here for Dev. Sound familiar?"

He grinned. "Nope."

She leaned her elbows on the counter across from him and smiled back. "Liar, liar, pants on fire."

"If the shoe fits." He shrugged. "What else have you been up to?"

"I picked up my brochures and advertising materials, and I've been mailing them out to big travel agencies across the country."

"Any response from the newspaper article?" he asked, then took a long swallow from his beer.

"Major response. I mailed a thank-you note to Annie and Walt," she said. "I've got both long summer holiday weekends completely booked. Various weeks in between are reserved, too. I'm even getting reservations for fall and winter."

Her eyes sizzled with excitement like sparklers on the Fourth of July. The only time she'd looked more beautiful to him was when he'd surprised her in the tub, wearing nothing but bubbles, pink cheeks and a smile.

"Good." Wimp word. A weak reaction for a woman who was well on her way. But if he said more than that one word, he couldn't hide the deep rasp of need he knew would creep into his voice.

He wanted to grab her around the waist and dance her through the house in celebration. But his reaction to thoughts of her and roots and home and telling her about his day raised his guard faster than a prairie fire with a tailwind.

"Thanks, Mitch."

"For what?"

"Your recommendation. Getting Annie out here. I don't for one minute believe it was about the championships. Publicity for a rodeo event spreads by osmosis just through the kids who compete, their folks and friends. Not to mention the local Texas sports pages. You kept your word to give me some good PR and there's no doubt in my mind that it helped."

"You're welcome."

"In spite of the past, everything that happened, you did what you said."

"You thought I wouldn't?"

"Not for a minute."

"*You're* a fibber," he said, tossing her words back at her.

"Not me. You're a good man and I appreciate it."

But he noticed that she kept the kitchen counter between them. He couldn't blame her for that or any doubts she might have about him, either. He wasn't in her league and never would be, no matter how much money he made.

Still, an almost overwhelming urge came over him to reach out and touch her, pull her around the barrier between them and into his arms. He wanted to storm her defenses and get her to lower the gate. To let him in, for her and himself, too. But he'd tried the relationship thing twice and been stomped into the dirt both times. Did he dare go for number three? Could he risk it again? Did he even want to chance having his feelings handed back to him?

Taylor had just thanked him for not holding a grudge about what had happened ten years ago. There was no point; he didn't care anymore. Not about Jen.

But Jen had been his first and most difficult lesson. Her message to him: he wasn't good enough for a woman he cared about to love him back. He wanted to believe he was a fair man, but damn it all, Taylor was Jen's sister. He'd said it himself—the fruit didn't fall far from the tree. Why should he believe she was different?

Her father hadn't liked him. Mitch was an abandoned kid from the wrong side of the tracks, and the man had found ways to remind him—hold it against him. Like father, like daughters? After leaving Destiny, he'd become a big-money winner on the pro rodeo circuit, and the buckle bunnies had lined up like competitors waiting for their shot. The lesson: women had hated or loved him and basically judged him not for who he was, but his status.

All except Taylor. Only, she'd been a girl then. But she was a woman now, and every painful lesson he'd ever learned came roaring back.

Taylor set her elbows on the counter, then rested her chin in her palm. "You look tired, Mitch. Tell me what you've been up to today," she said. "I know you don't want to discuss it, but give me the high points. The light version."

He found he wanted to tell her, just like ten years ago when he'd also claimed he didn't want to talk to her.

He let out a long breath. "I spent several hours in front of the Destiny City Council trying to convince them to change the zoning so my company could build a shopping center. I tried to convince them that their wives and daughters would be forever grateful to have stores in their own backyard. Come to think of it, maybe that wasn't the best strategy."

"I think it would be great. Now we have to go a long way or use catalogs to shop. If they agree, does that mean you'll be around for a while?"

"Yeah."

She turned away to pull plates out of the cupboard. He couldn't see her face to read her expression. Would she want him around? How would she feel if he stayed? He found the idea of basing his company in Destiny didn't make him want to catch the first bus out of town. In fact, the longer he was here, the better he liked the notion.

Ten years ago when he'd left, he'd put all his energy into bull riding, then his education and business. He'd worked hard at forgetting his life here. And that included Taylor.

Since coming back, he'd remembered the bad times, but there were good memories, too. Like the way he'd looked forward to describing for Taylor a particularly great ride on one of her father's bulls. He'd enjoyed telling her what happened to him at school. And when children's services had given him the bad news on his eighteenth birthday that he was on his own and no longer eligible for state assistance, Taylor had been the one he'd sought out to talk to. She hadn't let him down, either. She'd helped him find a room to rent and kept after her father to give him more work hours so he could pay for it. He'd thought their friendship was habit, or just the fact that she was always hanging around. But now he wasn't so sure. He *still* felt that connection with her, the sensation that he could tell her about anything. Except…

He recalled that night. Fourteen-year-old Taylor had tried to tag along with him and his friends to the lake. He'd brushed her off, and she'd been all horns and rattles and fit to be tied. As things turned out, it was probably the best decision he'd ever made. She was so young. She could have been the one…

But she wasn't. And the next night Jen had dumped him. He'd lashed out at Taylor—the only one who had never given him anything but friendship—and she'd said she loved him. Do you always hurt the ones you love?

There was no doubt she was a woman worth caring about, but love? He wasn't sure he knew what the word meant. Sure, he had feelings for her. But putting a label on them just wasn't something he wanted to risk.

"How do you feel about that?" She spooned chicken and vegetables over the rice she'd just put on the plates.

"Hmm? What?"

"About staying in Destiny?" she clarified.

"Would it bother you? After all, you're a former rodeo celebrity. Now you're a highfalutin businessman. Can you be happy hanging your hat in a one-horse town like this?"

She tried to joke, but the look in her eyes told him the answer mattered to her. One memory he wished he could erase was the look of hurt he'd seen on her face that night he'd pushed her away. He couldn't change the past, but he could do his best not to make the same mistakes. He wouldn't hurt her again. When his gaze strayed to her mouth, filling him with an almost uncontrollable yearning to kiss her, he turned away. A guy like him without roots and family ties couldn't help but hurt her.

If he'd been thinking straight, he'd have moved out right after he'd turned down Melissa Mae Arbrook's blatant invitation. Right then he'd known something was wrong. Instead he'd come back to the ranch to a naked, bubble-covered Taylor and kissed her. Although not when she was naked, which he had a feeling he would regret till his dying day. Because the weeks since then had only worked to make him want her until it was a constant ache inside him. Contrast and compare—what it felt like to have her, what it felt like to not. Having her was definitely better, but not especially smart.

He had tried to keep his feelings for Taylor under the heading brotherly, but hadn't managed to do that since he'd laid eyes on her again. But it was never too late. Meaning he'd better not kiss her like a lover. Better yet, not at all. If he laid a hand on her, he didn't think he could keep from kissing her senseless. Or touching her until she moaned with passion. Those seductive little noises in her throat made him burn for her until he thought he would go up in flames.

"Mitch? You're really zoning out tonight. You must really be tired."

"I guess so."

"How do you feel about the possibility of staying in Destiny?" She met his gaze and her own was hopeful.

Now's your chance, Rafferty. A golden opportunity to be noble and not hurt her. Be impersonal. He took a deep breath. "I'll do whatever I have to do to make my company a success," he said carefully.

Her eyes flickered with what might be disappointment, then the look was gone. "No one understands better than me the need to make a success of a business." She carried the plates into the dining room.

"Do you hear anything from Jen?" he asked.

He'd merely wanted to change the subject, but the look she shot him was anything but casual. In fact, it was a lot like her wounded-puppy look, the one he wished he could forget.

"I talk to her almost every day," she said.

Taylor hoped she hadn't sounded defensive. If so, she couldn't help it. At the mention of her sister's name, she'd almost dropped the plates she was holding. She hadn't been prepared for the question. Mitch hadn't talked about Jen since he'd first arrived. She'd thought...

What? That Mitch cared for *her?* That he wanted her? That the two times he'd kissed her had erased all those years of his wanting her sister? Apparently there was no statute of limitations on stupidity. Where Mitch Rafferty was concerned, she was destined to make a fool of herself for the rest of her life.

"How is she?" he asked.

"Who?"

"Jen." He sat down at a right angle to her and shot her a quizzical look. "Now who's zoning out? You must be tired," he said, using the same words she had.

"I am." Zoning out and tired, but not for the reason he thought.

Since the night he'd seen her in the tub, he'd worn his indifference like a comfortable pair of chaps. No matter how much she might want to, she couldn't blame him for putting her at arm's length. She'd always seen through his prickly exterior to his softhearted center. Apparently he was still a nice guy. The kind of man who had been hurt and wasn't about to turn around and do the same to a woman who had experienced heartbreak times two.

He'd kept his distance. A fact for which she was grateful. Really.

Okay. Maybe a time or two she'd wished Mitch would kiss her again. In an instant of spinelessness, she'd wanted just one more moment in his arms. But he hadn't approached her. Their interaction had been friendly but cool. And that was the devil of it. After her busted engagement, she'd made peace with the fact that she was meant to be alone.

Until Mitch walked back into her life.

Seeing him again had made her wonder, *What if?* Sharing a house together had given her a chance to see what a relationship with him could be like. She'd discovered it was pretty darn nice.

Then out of the blue he'd asked about Jen. And in a single instant, hopes she hadn't even realized she'd harbored popped, poofed and evaporated. Because she suddenly got it.

He hadn't gotten over her sister.

Not in ten years.

What would he say if he knew Jen was coming back for rodeo week? Was she coming because she knew Mitch was here?

Maybe it was for the best that they see each other again. Since he'd returned, she'd had a sense of forces from the past working on the present to make amends. Was she losing her mind? Next thing she knew, she'd start humming the theme from *The Twilight Zone*. But maybe it was time for Mitch and Jen to get together, the way it should have been ten years ago.

Taylor was fine about it. Only someone truly gifted in the art of idiocy would let her heart be broken by the same man twice. So it was no skin off her nose. Definitely for the best. And when pigs flew, she might almost believe that.

But there was no point in not telling him. "Jen will be here tomorrow."

Chapter Nine

"It will be good to see her again," Mitch said evenly.

Taylor watched him carefully for signs that he still cared for her sister. Since she'd recently experienced symptoms of seeing the guy she'd had a thing for ten years ago, she knew what to look for. Shortness of breath, keen interest manifested by a glow inside so powerful that it must be visible on the outside, too, trembling hands, nervous energy, sweaty palms.

He showed none of the above.

But the man had made his fortune riding bulls. He had nerves of steel. Of course he would be able to hide his reaction.

Maybe she could provoke one. "Jen's been busy. A heavy caseload at work. I haven't seen much of her. It will be good to have her here," she said.

"So you *do* get lonely," he teased.

"As you've pointed out on several occasions, I do talk to myself, so I guess that's a logical assumption." She picked up her fork and met his gaze. "But it's not loneliness in the usual sense. I'm perfectly content on the ranch. But I'm social, too. I can't deny that it's nice to have someone besides myself to talk to."

He frowned. "How come you never married, Taylor?"

She was still watching him, searching for a signal that he couldn't wait to see Jen again. For the second, time he'd caught her off guard with a question. Not to mention that he boomeranged attention from Jen back to herself. Perverse man. What did that mean? Confusion caused her to consider the question for several moments before answering.

"I already told you why," she finally said. "I was engaged and it didn't work out." She shrugged. "End of story."

He shook his head. "There are any number of available guys for a social belle like yourself."

"Like who?"

"Grady O'Connor, for instance."

"He's got his hands full with twin girls." She laughed. "He's said more than once the last thing he needs is another female in his life. In fact, the girls picked out a new pup recently at the animal shelter in Destiny, and Grady insisted it be a boy."

"Okay," he said, but his tone implied he didn't believe that for a second. "Then what about Dev Hart?"

"More than one meddler in town has tried to fix me up with him. Including but not limited to Bonnie Potts and Doc Holloway."

"I'm not surprised. You two have a lot in common. You could do worse."

"I could do better. But yagottawanna. And I don't want to."

"Why? He's not bad-looking."

"You noticed that, did you?" she asked with a grin. She pulled a mantle of teasing and nonchalance around her to cover up the hurt. Was this nice guy Mitch Rafferty? Was he trying to pair her with someone else so it wouldn't hurt like the devil tomorrow when he took up with her sister again?

"I'm on the lookout for *you,*" he answered pointedly, unruffled by her teasing. "He's got money. Nice house. Cute kid. What's not to like?"

"Easy question, not even a challenge. Dev isn't over his ex-wife. I already had a bad experience with a rebound Romeo. Why would

I trade a wonderful friendship for a doomed romance with Dev?"

"So you wouldn't be alone."

"I'm not going there. I found out that if the someone in your life doesn't make it better, then there's something wrong. I'm way past the age where a woman needs a man to feel fulfilled."

"You're too young to be way past any age."

"Okay. Then I'm at the 'if it ain't broke, don't fix it' stage."

"Is that the one where dating is too much trouble?"

"That's the one," she agreed. "Partly. The engagement fiasco happened because I overlooked the college fiasco—"

"What?" he asked sharply.

She wondered at the intensity of his expression, not to mention the bite in his tone. "It was no big deal. I think every girl runs into a guy like that. If she's smart, it's only once."

"A guy like what?" He encircled her wrist with a steely grip, not hurtful but enough to get her attention. His gaze said he wouldn't put up with evasion.

"Oh, you know the type. He thinks he's God's gift and a woman should count herself lucky if he condescends to toss her a crumb of attention. But I didn't realize that at first.

I cared about him a lot. Right up until he wanted something I wasn't prepared to give."

"What did he do?" he demanded, slightly increasing the pressure of his grip. Anger sizzled in his blue eyes.

"He got pushy, said he'd waited long enough. I was a tease. And he wouldn't take no for an answer."

"He didn't—"

She shook her head. "I backed him off with the move you showed me. A well-placed knee, issued in a businesslike way, is pretty convincing."

He looked at her for a moment, then his mouth turned up at the corners into a pleased grin. "It worked?"

"Like a charm." She returned his smile. "He called me some ugly names, but his gasping soprano took out the sting. And he said I should loosen up if I didn't want to be alone, that guys only want one thing."

"Son of a b—" He stopped and took a deep breath. "A lot of guys do, Taylor. But not all."

"What do the others want?"

"Success, stability, a family, friends they can count on. A place to call home. Everyone needs to figure out what it is they're looking for."

"Have you?"

But she already knew the answer. He'd been looking for ten years and he still wanted Jen.

He shook his head. "I haven't figured that out yet. But when I do, you'll be the first to know."

She wouldn't have to wait longer than tomorrow, she thought. And one picture was worth a thousand words. He would only have to take one look at Jen. Taylor would be able to read him like a book. She would know and he wouldn't have to say a single word.

THE FINAL PREPARATIONS were under way for the championships that night. Mitch stood by the fence, supervising assembly of the spectator grandstands. A huge tarp had been erected to provide shade from the June sun. Hannah Morgan's medical trailer was in place behind the arena, close by in case it was needed, which he hoped it wouldn't be. A stand to sell refreshments was set up in a convenient location to the activities and viewers. He was counting on folks to come hungry, because profits would go to the rodeo association. Beside that, a booth had been erected to market souvenir T-shirts and programs—another source of revenue that would go to the kids. Maggie Benson had agreed to man that stall in order to advertise This 'n That, her successful clothing, antiques and country-crafts shop in downtown Destiny. He'd seen some of her hand-embroidered denim jackets and knew she was a true artist, not to mention pretty cute, which wouldn't hurt sales.

In the distance, he could see the crew working on chalking out a parking area for the friends, family and rodeo supporters who would attend the week's activities. He nodded with satisfaction. Everything seemed to be falling into place.

But this whole complicated production was a walk in the park compared to the monumental chore of putting Taylor out of his mind.

He heard footsteps behind him and his Taylor-radar cranked up, kick-starting his heart. Part of him was pumping his arm and shouting yee-haw; the other part groaned in frustration. How was he going to learn to treat her like a little sister after he'd kissed her like a lover?

"Hi, Mitch." She stepped on the first rung of the fence beside him and crossed her arms on the top. She was so close he could smell her fragrance and knew that she'd used cucumber-melon body lotion.

"Hi," he answered through gritted teeth.

Glancing at him, she said, "You look like the seventh dwarf, Grumpy. What's wrong?"

"Not a thing, little T." He deliberately used Dev's nickname for her. She'd assured him that the stockman was nothing more than her friend. That was almost the same as a big brother. He would imitate Dev to keep her at a distance.

She frowned, and the expression on her face said she was puzzled. But all she said was "Smile when you call me that."

"How are things up at the house? Guests settled in okay?"

He had arranged for some of the rodeo association's board of directors to stay on the ranch. Not only was it convenient for them, but there were several influential members who could help her operation by word of mouth.

She nodded. "The place is full, except my old room. So far I've heard nothing but raves. I think the folks you recommended will really help. Thanks for giving me the business."

That wasn't the business he wanted to give her, but no way could he tell her that. "I'm glad it's working out. It's the least the board can do. Thanks to you, there's going to be a rodeo for these kids."

"No, thanks to you. I provided the land. But every invasion needs a general."

He grinned. "I like that. General Mitch Rafferty."

"I suspect I'm asking the impossible, but don't let it go to your head."

"With you around? Not a chance."

"I'm not going anywhere." She shot him a challenging look as if to say, *Are you?*

After several moments, she turned to study the preparations in progress. He took the opportunity to memorize the sight of her. Her white straw hat sat squarely on her head, casting a shadow over her face, shielding her from the brutal Texas sun. Most of her hair was tucked up and off her neck, except for the wisps that refused to surrender and danced around her face in the breeze. Her cute little turned-up nose was pink and peeling and sported a hodgepodge of freckles, an occupational hazard of working outside. But with her B and B on the verge of off and running, she would probably split her time indoors and out.

She wore a light blue denim shirt tucked into worn jeans that showed off her curves to mouthwatering perfection. It would be so easy to slip his arm around her slender waist and snuggle her against him. He'd discovered that she fit there perfectly. Now he struggled to forget that fact.

"It's exciting, isn't it?" she asked.

He nodded. "Some of the best memories I've got are from high school rodeo."

"Hmm," she said wistfully. "Do you miss the pros, too?"

He nodded. "There's an excitement, an underlying humming that sets every muscle and nerve ending on edge. It's a high that you can't get any other way. That's what I miss most."

"Even after all this time?" she asked.

"I think it will be with me until I'm a hundred and five."

"A hundred and five? That's ambitious." She flashed him a smile that went straight to his heart.

"The spirit is willing, and always will be," he said. "But the flesh— Well, that's another kettle of fish."

"Or a horse of a different color," she commented, giving him a wry look.

He laughed. "A bull of a different shade would be more accurate. I'd like nothing better than to partake of the bone-rattling event. Unfortunately my bones are a lot older now. And I like to think I'm wise enough to protect them from myself."

"Meaning old age is hot on your heels," she teased.

"Meaning I'm *almost* content to leave it to the youngsters." He considered the wistful expression on her face. "What about you, Grandma Moses?"

"What about me?" she asked, slanting him a saucy look.

He recalled how she'd looked when she'd told him why she hadn't rodeoed since the championships ten years ago. At the time, he'd had the feeling that there was more to it than what she'd told him, about her father's lack of support. His recollection of her dad was that he backed his girls in whatever endeavor they chose. If Mitch was right, then Taylor was the one who had decided to quit competing. As much promise as she'd shown, he couldn't help wondering why.

"Do you miss competing?" he asked.

"Some of my best memories are of high school competition," she answered, parroting what he'd said moments before.

"You were so fast, so skilled, so focused. I don't think I've ever seen a horsewoman with more promise than you. Why did you quit? And I'm not buying the lame excuse you gave me. Your dad was a rancher. He boarded rodeo stock."

"That's just business."

"Okay. But he was also a proud father. I may not know a lot about families or a parent's pride, but I saw the look on his face when you rode. He didn't look like a man who couldn't care less about his daughter's activities. What's the real reason, Taylor?"

She met his gaze with her own shadowed, doubtful look. After mumbling something that sounded a lot like "What harm can it do?" she said, "I miss the excitement. I loved the thrill that sang through me when I woke up in the morning on the day of the events. The adrenaline rush as I waited my turn, mentally calculating every move I'd make, was like nothing I've experienced before or since. I enjoyed the challenge of trying to stay loose, to keep my horse loose so I could anticipate any moves he might make."

He stared at her. "So why did you stop?"

"Jen eloped."

"What did that have to do with you?"

She shrugged, then squinted across the arena to the preparations in progress. "And you went away. Nothing was the same. I guess the fun went out of it for me."

"Do you ever wish you could go back to the way things were?"

"All the time," she said.

"Not me."

"Why not? You had girls hanging around you three deep. What's not to like?" Then she nodded knowingly, but there was a tension in her body language. When she met his gaze, her own was shuttered. "This is about Jen."

Her voice lacked emotion, but somehow he knew that was deliberate.

"Partly," he admitted. "But my feelings for her ended a long time ago. I put it in the 'no pain, no gain' category."

"So you admit she hurt you?"

"I never denied that. And you should know that better than anyone. But I learned from what happened with her. School of hard knocks has always been my best education."

"And the lesson?"

"Don't compete when you haven't got a chance."

"So when my sister gets here this evening, you expect to feel nothing?"

He didn't miss the edge in her voice or how she studied him like the notes for her last college final. "That's right. Like I said, I stopped caring about Jen years ago."

"Not even a twinge of the old feelings?"

"Nope."

"She's better-looking than she was ten years ago."

"Most people are. Including you," he pointed out. "Please tell me you're not playing match-maker."

She shook her head. "It's just that I've got this feeling—"

"What?" he asked when she hesitated.

"You're going to laugh, but ever since you returned to Destiny, I can't help feeling as if the past is clamoring to be organized and set to rights."

"That sounds like something out of a science-fiction movie," he said, laughing.

"I knew you wouldn't take me seriously. But Jen is beautiful, sophisticated and fun. She's an up-and-coming family law attor-ney—"

"Speaking of cross-examinations," he in-terrupted. "Is there a point to yours anywhere in my future?" It sounded as if she was trying to sell him on her sister. For the life of him, he couldn't figure out why.

"I just can't help wondering if you really meant what you said."

"About what?" he asked.

"When you see Jensen again, will you be lying when you said you feel nothing? That you stopped caring for her years ago?"

"I don't have to see her. I can tell you right now I was lying."

"You were?" She looked surprised and there was almost a stricken expression on her face.

"Yeah. I expect when I see Jen I'll feel the pleasure of getting reacquainted with an old friend."

"Yeah, and longhorns will fly."

She stepped off her perch and stuck her hands into her pockets. Turning away without another word, she walked down the slight hill toward the house, shoulders slumped.

He wanted to follow and pull her into his arms. But he didn't dare. He wouldn't hurt her for the world. Besides the fact that she was all about home, family, roots and he had no experience with any of the above, he needed to put the past to rest. He'd never felt about any woman the way he felt about Taylor. But he had unfinished business with her sister.

He was almost positive the spark for Jensen was dead, but she was his first love, the first woman he'd wanted.

Tomorrow he would know.

Chapter Ten

Standing at Taylor's front door with Grady O'Connor, Mitch saw the sweet, sporty red BMW convertible raising dust clouds as it raced down the long dirt road. It passed the chalked-off rodeo parking, then rounded the arena area and headed for the house. Championships were due to start in about two hours, he noted, glancing at his watch. Spectators would be showing up soon.

"Looks like someone's navigational system is haywire," he commented to Grady.

Through his reflective aviator sunglasses, the sheriff studied the vehicle coming toward them. "I can handle this. That's why you're paying me the big bucks."

Mitch grinned. "By definition, *volunteer* means you don't get paid. And that was your choice. But I gotta tell you, buddy, it'd be tough to retire on that. There's money in the rodeo budget for security."

"My deputies deserve every bit of that. I'm just here to supervise."

"And spectate," Mitch clarified.

"And set wayward ladies straight," he added, nodding in the direction of the luxury car that had just come to a stop.

"The top is up on that convertible, and the windows are tinted. How do you know that's a woman driver?" Mitch asked, intrigued.

"Gut feeling. The car. The color. I've done a personal, unofficial study. Besides, I'm a cop. After a while, we law-enforcement types get an instinct about this sort of thing."

"When do you find the time for any study— official or otherwise?" Mitch asked, remembering Melissa Mae Arbrook's words about him sheriffing, ranching and parenting twin girls.

"So you think I'm wrong?" he countered, neatly sidestepping the question.

"It's not that. I just—"

"If you doubt my expertise, just wait a second," he said, nodding toward the car.

The door opened and two slender, tanned legs appeared. The hem of her—and it was definitely a her—lime-green sundress hiked up to reveal a shapely thigh. Impractical brown leather sandals revealed her feet and toenails painted pink. A memory flashed, hitting Mitch with a vision of Taylor's pink-painted toes propped on the side of the tub. Heat radiated through him, followed by a niggling sensation of familiarity.

When the woman finally emerged from the car, he guessed she was about Taylor's height, which meant not very tall. But she had a whole lot of slender and shapely packed into her compact figure. Her brown hair, highlighted with red, dusted the back of her bare neck and just the tops of her shoulders.

Mitch knew who she was. He glanced at Grady, wondering if he'd recognized her yet. In spite of the sunglasses, he noted an expression on the other man's face that indicated he liked what he saw.

Grady looked at Mitch. Together they said, "Jensen."

"How did you know?" Mitch asked. He had dated her once upon a time. But he was surprised that the sheriff was able to identify her from the back.

"She doesn't look like a typical rodeo spectator," Grady observed. "No jeans, hat or boots."

"Inconclusive. At an event like this, there are a lot of people who don't dress the part. What was your real clue?"

Grady grinned, flashing white teeth against

the tanned skin of his face. "Best legs I've ever seen, bar none."

He moved forward to greet her. Smiling and shaking his head, Mitch followed.

"Excuse me, ma'am," Grady said in his cool, polite cop voice. "This is private parking for the Stevens family and guests of the ranch. Unless you're expected—"

Jensen turned. Designer sunglasses covered her eyes, but Mitch remembered they were moss-green. Emotions crossed her face in rapid succession—annoyance, surprise, then recognition. Something about the upward curve of her mouth told him she was going to give the sheriff a hard time. And he knew Grady's remote expression was nothing more than law-enforcement training. But he felt his friend's air of expectation and waited for that to bother him. It didn't.

He wondered how long it had been since the two of them had seen each other. They were both busy professionals, but Grady had based a positive identification on a pair of dynamite legs. Mitch's recognition had been more subtle. Taylor had told him she was arriving sometime today, but with all the last-minute details to attend to, the fact had slipped his mind. Then that damn, sexy pink toenail polish the Stevens sisters seemed to favor had given him the defining clue.

Somehow on Taylor it was more seductive, probably because it was so unexpected. If he hadn't seen it for himself, he'd never have guessed that beneath her cotton blouse, worn denim and scuffed work boots lurked those luscious pink-painted toes and a tempting body to go with them. Heat seared him at the thought but he pulled himself back with an effort.

"Unless I'm expected? A girl likes being *unexpected,* Sheriff," Jensen was saying. "But that's not what you meant, is it?"

"No, ma'am."

"What makes you think no one is expecting me?" she asked, lifting her chin.

"The rooms are full up."

Mitch knew for a fact that there was an empty one across from his that Taylor had saved for her sister.

Grady rested his hands on his hips. "I suggest you move your car."

"It's awfully heavy—"

"Getting smart isn't the way to win friends and influence the sheriff," he said, cutting her off.

"I can't help it. I was born that way." She grinned, showing off her dazzling smile.

"C'mon, Grady. I thought a Texas sheriff had a courtly image to uphold."

Mitch could almost see her batting her eyelashes behind those dark glasses. He stood back and watched the sparks fly.

Grady removed his own sunglasses and smiled. "Okay, Counselor. You win."

"I should hope so, Grady O'Connor."

"Seriously, Jen, that expensive model is a car-thief magnet. There'll be a lot of strangers milling around for the next few days. In my professional opinion, you should park it out of sight."

She nodded. "Why didn't you just say so, Sheriff?"

"Just havin' a little fun."

"You? Fun?" she asked, tipping her head to the side. "Rumor has it you don't have time for it."

"Rumor?"

Mitch and Grady looked at each other and said together, "Melissa Mae Arbrook."

She laughed and said, "I stopped at the Road Kill Café on my way here. She said to tell you hi." Then Jensen met Mitch's gaze. "Hello, stranger."

He hesitated a couple of beats before holding out his hand. "Jen, it's good to see you. I think Taylor was expecting you a little later."

"You knew she was coming?" Grady asked.

"Yeah."

"You could have jumped in anytime and clued me in."

"It didn't take you long to figure out who she was," Mitch pointed out. "Besides, I didn't want to interfere with your unofficial study, your gut feeling in action. It was pretty impressive."

Jen's curious gaze jumped back and forth between them. "And just how did you figure out it was me?"

"The classy, shapely, stacked—wheels," Grady finally said. "Nice car."

"Oh. Thanks."

Grady put his sunglasses back on. "It's good to see you again, Jen. But I need to get to work. Catch you two later."

"Count on it," she answered.

He politely touched the brim of his tan sheriff's hat and walked away.

Jen watched his back for several moments, then looked at the house. "I can't wait to see what Taylor's done with the place."

"You haven't seen it yet?"

"Not completely finished. My job is in Dallas and I'm pretty busy. I don't get home as often as I'd like."

Home. That four-letter word again. In the

weeks he'd been there, he felt the pull of it. Taylor had singlehandedly made him think about putting down roots, about being part of a family.

"Let's go inside. I'll get your bag."

"Thanks," she said and unlocked her trunk.

Mitch lifted several suitcases out. "You moving back in?" he asked.

"I'm taking some time off," she answered vaguely.

He nodded, then walked with her up the steps and into the air-conditioned house. Jen wandered through the downstairs. "She's done wonders with the place."

"I'll take these to your room."

"Okay."

They climbed the stairs, and Jen poked her head into every nook and cranny to assess the changes her sister had made. At the end of the hall, Mitch turned to his right and set her luggage in the room Taylor had slept in. He still felt the ache of missing her.

Jen studied him. "So... It's been a long time."

"Yeah, it has," he said, tucking his fingertips in the front pockets of his jeans as he leaned against the door frame.

Mitch realized for the next week, until the championships were over, he would be shar-

ing a bathroom with Jensen Stevens. This was
the definitive test. Ten years ago he would
have sold his soul for the opportunity. He
looked at her now and waited for lightning
to strike.

Nothing.

Just a warm pleasure at seeing an old friend.
He would never have known her legs anywhere, but he'd noticed the sparks between her
and Grady O'Connor. He waited for jealousy
to settle like a hot coal in his gut.

Nothing.

He would know jealousy. Lately he'd had
a taste of it—more like an all-you-can-eat
buffet. Taylor talking with Dev Hart. Taylor
standing between the good-looking stockman and Grady O'Connor for those publicity photos. Even now the memories burned
a jealous streak as bright and hot as a black-
smith's forge after he got done with the bel-
lows. It made him crazy that either of those
men would be good for her. But damn it,
Mitch couldn't stand the idea of losing Taylor to anyone.

"Taylor told me you were back." Jen put her
hand on his arm. "But she didn't say much
else. How are you?"

"Fine. I hear you're an up-and-comer in the
law business."

She nodded. "Daddy always said I argued like a lawyer, I should go to school so I could make some money at it."

"I guess he was right."

"I can't help wondering if—"

"What?" he encouraged. He had a feeling he knew what she was going to say. "If Zach hadn't died, you wouldn't have gone back to school?"

Looking uncomfortable, she ran a hand through her long, dark hair. Finally she nodded. "How did you know?"

"Ever since I came back, the past has been dogging my heels." He recalled Taylor saying almost the same thing. He'd laughed, just as she'd predicted, but now he knew what she meant. And he had to admit she was right.

It was as if his return had triggered something cosmic, set forces in motion to fix what had gone wrong in the past. Only, he would bet everything he had that he'd never been meant to wind up with Jensen. Since coming back to Destiny, he'd found there was always a memory waiting in the wings to catch him off guard. But they were all about Taylor.

Jen looked at him now and her green eyes were filled with remorse. "I've thought about you often, Mitch."

"And what did you think?"

"I wished that I'd told you how much I regret what happened."

What happened was that she'd wasted herself on a guy who wasn't good enough for her. But there was no point in speaking ill of the dead. Or destroying her illusions.

"Don't worry about it," he said.

"I regret hurting you."

"That was a long time ago."

"Yes, and it's way past time for me to set the record straight. The truth is, I wasn't seeing Zach behind your back. We were friends. We flirted a little. I was too young to realize that I was playing with fire, and that night at the championships it all exploded out of control. I didn't plan it or deliberately cheat on you. It all—" she spread her hands wide in a gesture of helplessness "—just happened."

"Forget it."

"I fell head over heels in love with Zach. I can't be sorry for one perfect year with the love of my life. But that doesn't justify hurting you, especially the way you found out. I don't want to lose your friendship."

"Do you need me to tell you it's okay?"

Biting the corner of her bottom lip, she nodded uncertainly.

"Consider it done. It's over, Jen. I'm okay. And now I have something to ask you."

"Anything. I owe you."

"How did you know it was love? With Zach," he asked.

There was a faraway expression in her green eyes and he knew she was pulling up the memories and sifting through them. "I remember the exact moment when I knew beyond a shadow of a doubt."

He laughed. "Spoken like a lawyer. When was that?"

"Melissa Mae Allen was flirting with Zach. Outrageously teasing and toying with him. It made me so crazy that I wanted to deck her."

"Why didn't you?"

"I was rodeo queen. I had an image to pro-tect," she said sheepishly, shaking her head. "But I was so angry. I felt like I was losing him and I had to do something about it."

"Yeah," he said, knowing Zach was the type of guy who would use that to his ad-vantage.

"It was good and right between Zach and me," she said, her cheeks going rosy in spite of an echo of defensiveness in her tone. "But I wish I'd had a chance to talk to you before everything got crazy. I handled it badly. My only defense is that I was young."

"That's one of those character-building

experiences your father was always talking about."

She smiled sadly. "He did go on about that, didn't he?" She sighed. "I just want to say again that I'm sorry. It's ten years too late, and way past time I told you that, but I hope you'll accept my apology."

"Okay. Can we be finished with it now?"

"Absolutely." She looked relieved. "So is there anyone special in your life?"

Your sister.

The thought came instantly. For a moment he was afraid he'd said it out loud. But her quizzical expression didn't change to shock or disapproval. "Define special."

Without hesitation she said, "Taylor."

Bull's-eye, he thought. But Mitch knew that it was pointless to admit that he was in love. He was wrong for Taylor. Her father had made it clear he wasn't good enough for Jensen. Just because Mitch loved a different daughter didn't mean the man would change his mind.

"Who would want an old Texas tumbleweed like me?" he asked, desperate to change the subject.

"A better, easier question is—what living, breathing woman wouldn't?" she said, laughing.

There was only one woman he wanted to want him. But she was filet mignon; he was hamburger. He cared too much to drag her down to his level.

He shook his head. "No. I'm a loner—always was, always will be."

"You don't still have a chip on your shoulder, do you?"

"Hey, this is me," he said, trying to grin.

"Yeah, I know." Her green eyes seemed to laser straight into his soul. "Do you need me to tell you *you're* okay?"

"It's not your job."

"But someone's got to do it or you'll blow a good thing with my sister."

"What makes you think—"

She held up her hand. "It doesn't take a mental giant. You've been here for several weeks under the same roof. I talk to her almost every day. I can read between the lines. Besides—"

"What?" he asked.

"You never talked to me the way you did to Taylor. You never opened up with me like you did with her. More than once I came downstairs after getting ready for our date and I'd hear the two of you talking about all kinds of things. And laughing. With me you were intense and closed-off."

He shrugged. "It was easy to talk to Taylor. I didn't feel like I had to impress her. I didn't have to be good enough. Until now," he added softly, and not for her to hear.

"Dad's gone," she said, meeting his gaze with a look that told him she had heard. "As the eldest member of the family, it *is* my job to tell you you're okay. If he were here, I know he would say he'd been wrong about you. He would tell you that you're a good man and proudly welcome you to the family."

"Do you really believe that?" he asked, hoping it was the truth.

"With all my heart. For the record," she said, "you're more than okay."

Years of self-doubt began to melt away. That chip on his shoulder as big as Texas fell off. He finally felt free.

He nodded, then let out a long breath. "What about you? Anyone special in your life?"

A sad expression turned her moss-colored eyes a darker shade of green. "I had my shot at love. It was wonderful while it lasted. But I guess one year is all destiny meant for me to have."

"There hasn't been anyone else?" Taylor had told him as much. But it was hard to believe a woman as beautiful as Jen hadn't had another relationship.

She shook her head and smiled, but it was sad around the edges. "I never wanted anyone else." She met his gaze and rested her hand on his forearm. "Don't worry about me, Mitch."

"I'm not."

"Prevaricator."

"You think I don't know you just called me a liar?" he asked, his mouth curving up in a reluctant smile.

She laughed. "You're good. And you're a nice man. I don't deserve it after what I did to you. But I guess what goes around comes around."

"You and I were kid stuff, Jen. Losing Zach was not your punishment for what happened. It was just one of those things."

"If you say so."

Mitch ran his hand through his hair. "I have to ask. Would you do the same thing again? Marry Zach, I mean."

"In a heartbeat." She released a big sigh. "Except I wouldn't hurt you like I did. But with all my heart I believe that it's better to have loved and lost than to never have loved at all. So don't be an idiot. Tell Taylor how you feel."

"Yes, ma'am," he said, taking her hands

and giving them a friendly squeeze. "The guy who gets you is going to be one lucky son of a gun. Thanks, Jen."

He leaned down and kissed her cheek, then pulled her into his arms for a brotherly bear hug. In that moment, he knew. He'd come face-to-face with his past and looked it square in the eye. It didn't have power over him anymore. He wanted roots, home, family—with Taylor. As soon as he saw her—

Distantly he heard the sound of boots at the end of the upstairs hall. "I saw your car, Jen. Where the heck are you hiding?" That was Taylor's voice.

Before he could back away from Jen, he heard a sharp intake of breath. He turned just in time to see the sparkle die in Taylor's eyes. He quickly dropped his arms to his sides. "Taylor."

"I'm sorry. I didn't mean to interrupt," she said, not looking at him.

"You weren't. We were just discussing old times." Jensen smiled. "Hi, little sister." She opened her arms and the two hugged. There was no mistaking the fierce and genuine affection they shared.

Mitch envied that. The only feeling he'd had that was even close was the bond he had shared with Dev, Grady and Jack back in high school. He couldn't imagine brothers being closer than the four of them. He couldn't imagine a closer relationship. Until now—until Taylor.

He saw the bruised expression in her eyes and wanted to assure her that he felt nothing romantic for Jen.

"Taylor, listen—"

"How was the drive up from Dallas?" she asked, cutting him off, not even looking in his direction.

"Long," Jen answered.

Taylor smiled, but it was phony and not enough to chase the shadows from her eyes. "So what's up? Are you two getting reacquainted?"

"Nothing more than old friends catching up," he said, knowing it wasn't enough.

"We've been talking about the past," Jen said.

"Anything you want to tell me?" Taylor asked, trying to make her voice light.

Mitch had something very important to tell her, but this wasn't the time or place. He had to do it right. He'd been given a "do over" and he was determined not to screw it up the way he had ten years ago. As soon as his responsibility to the rodeo was over, he planned to have a serious heart-to-heart with Miss Taylor Stevens. Wine, flowers and dinner at a very expensive restaurant would be involved.

He wanted to reassure her, but it would have to wait until they were alone and he could do it the way he wanted. Hot, wet kisses would definitely be involved. But he had a rodeo to kick off.

Mitch walked to the doorway. "I've got to get over to the arena and make sure everything is ready. I'll see you two later."

Taylor could almost hear her heart crack as Mitch disappeared. She was the world's biggest idiot. A three-time loser. She'd lost her fiancé to his first love and still that hadn't been enough to keep her from falling in love with Mitch all over again. Seeing her sister in his arms made her chest ache so much that she could hardly catch her breath. It was destiny. They were back together again.

Jensen put her hands on her hips. "Does he know yet?"

"What?"

"That you're in love with him."

"Nope." She realized she'd been cornered into all but admitting her feelings. Exasperated, Taylor glared at her sister. "I hate when you use your legal training. I'm not in love with Mitch."

"The way you look at him says differently.

I saw pictures of Zach and me together, and I looked at him exactly the same way."

"Zach loved you back," Taylor pointed out, trying to shift attention away from herself.

"Yeah."

The strained tone in Jen's voice made Taylor look more closely at her sister and the odd expression on her face. "Zach did love you, didn't he?"

Jen shook her head as if to clear away unwanted images. She smiled, but it was a little wobbly around the edges. "Of course he loved me. But we're talking about you and Mitch. If you're still in love with him, you have to tell him."

"Nope. I did that once. He told me I kiss like a little girl and I was as homely as a mud fence."

"He didn't!"

"Not exactly," Taylor admitted. "But the little-girl part is true."

"That was ten years ago. I'd bet the ranch that he feels differently now."

"You can't bet the ranch. It's mine. I bought you out," Taylor reminded her. "And I don't believe he feels differently at all."

He still loves you, she thought.

"You're not upset because he kissed me?"

She put her hands on her hips. "And that was nothing more than a bury-the-hatchet hug."

"I couldn't care less what you and Mitch do."

"Whoppers like that are going to send you straight to hell."

Speaking of whoppers, what hurt the most was that his heart-stopping, soul-stirring, toe-curling kisses had been a lie.

Jen shook her head. "I think Mitch might be in love with you."

"I think you're crazy."

"Wouldn't it be better to know for sure if he cares?"

Taylor *was* sure. She loved Mitch and he wanted her sister. And she'd been wrong. The heartache wasn't the same as she'd known ten years ago. It was ten times worse. Somehow she would have to find a way to survive it.

Jen met her gaze. "Love deeply and passionately. You might get hurt, but it's the only way to live life completely."

Taylor would have to learn to live life a lot *less* completely. "You should take your own advice, big sister."

"We're talking about you. I had my chance at happiness. And even knowing what I know now, I wouldn't change marrying Zach. A love like that only comes along once. Life is too short to miss opportunities."

"Life *is* too short," Taylor agreed, hoping that would make her sister drop the subject.

"Not only that, great love and great achievements involve great risk. You're on the threshold of both." Jen took her cosmetic bag into the bathroom. "I think I'll freshen up before we go to the rodeo."

Taylor shook her head when she was alone. Leave it to Jen to go from lofty ideals to the basics of great skin care. She respected her sister a great deal. But no way would she tell Mitch how she felt, knowing for sure how he felt about Jen.

For a moment, anger welled up in her. Jen had given him up. She'd handed her heart to another man and walked away. A fierce desire to fight for the man she loved grew inside Taylor. Then she remembered. The last time she'd done that, humiliation and heartache had been her reward. It was about time she learned from her mistakes, because she didn't think she could handle it if he rejected her again.

After seeing her sister in Mitch's arms, a ton of bucking bull couldn't convince her to bare her soul to him again. Ten years ago, Jen was everything he'd wanted.

"And I'm still just me," Taylor whispered to the empty room.

Chapter Eleven

Four days later on the last night of the rodeo, Taylor sat alone on the hard metal bleachers, watching the activity in an arena illuminated as bright as day by powerful spotlights. The smells of popcorn, peanuts, hot dogs and cotton candy mingled in the air around her while she watched the last team-roping duo compete. When the first rope fell short and the animal outran the second, she knew that Cal White and April Richter would take the event. She couldn't help being proud of two of her teen employees, and clapped excitedly when their names were announced as the winners.

Then she saw Mitch. When he walked into the center of the arena, she noticed he limped slightly. He must be tired. The thought tugged at her heart. And when her pulse skipped at the sight of him, she realized something. The Mitch Rafferty adrenaline rush was much more thrilling than anything she'd experienced while competing.

Although her heart was broken, she knew she would find the strength to go on. But the part of her that could care about any man but Mitch was frozen forever. It had disintegrated ten years ago, deactivated by a laser look from his bad-boy blue eyes.

"Folks, we're going to take a break while we have the tractor smooth out the arena for the barrel-racing and pole-bending events." Static from his microphone stopped him and he checked the tiny device clipped to his collar, then the small square contraption attached to his belt. "Better?" he asked, and a murmur of assent whispered through the crowd.

He proceeded to announce sportsmanship awards to a senior girl and boy, and a memorial scholarship. The overall point winners were named and the rookie cowboy and cowgirl. "And finally, I'd like to announce that this year's rodeo queen is April Richter. C'mon up here, April."

The blonde, cute-as-a-button girl quickly walked to the center of the arena and Mitch placed the traditional tiara over the crown of her black Stetson. She said something to him and he nodded.

"April would especially like to thank her

parents and the rest of her family for their support. Congratulations, April."

When the teenager walked away, Mitch continued, "There are some people I need to thank for helping me put this shindig together. The board of directors of the Texas High School Rodeo Association. Bonnie Potts organized the timers. Grady O'Connor provided security. Dev Hart, our stock contractor and pickup man."

The sound of his voice, the look of him, so tall, strong and confident in the spotlight, all conspired to make Taylor realize he was a perfect match for her sister. He had well and truly left her behind. Again—and for good this time. He didn't need her, and the realization was so painful it stole her breath. She stood and climbed down the stairs to the bottom of the bleachers.

"I'd also like to thank Taylor Stevens for opening the Circle S ranch to us. We'd have had this rodeo even if we had to shut down I-20. But it wouldn't have come off so well. Let's give Taylor a big hand before she gets away."

He'd been watching her! Before she could take that thought any further, a round of applause rang through the air. Cheeks warm with embarrassment, Taylor turned and waved to the crowd in the bleachers.

"Taylor is about to open the doors to her dude ranch. To show our appreciation for her help, let's spread the word about the best-kept secret in Texas—the Circle S, B and B Western-style. She wants to show as many folks as possible what traditional Western hospitality is all about. Show stressed-out city slickers what silence sounds like."

Static cut him off again, then the sound of tapping poured through the speakers. "Can you hear me now?"

The spectators nodded and murmured their agreement.

"I recommend anyone interested in a true Texas experience call the 800 number listed in the program and on the sign in the arena. She's taking reservations and they're going fast, folks."

Tears filled her eyes as Taylor walked quickly away from the spotlighted arena. The last thing she wanted to do was cry in public. Mitch had gone above and beyond the letter and spirit of their agreement. He'd gotten a story in the newspapers and publicly promoted her business. Somehow, this hurt more than his rejection a decade ago. She couldn't hide behind her anger. She had no resentment to coat her feelings and protect her. A sweet and considerate Mitch Rafferty hurt her most of all. Because she loved him and he would never return it.

As she brushed moisture from her cheeks, she almost didn't hear the female voice call to her.

"Taylor?"

She stopped and looked at her friend Maggie Benson, a petite, redheaded bundle of energy with a riot of curls around her pretty face. Maggie leaned a slender shoulder against the post of her booth, which displayed the official rodeo T-shirts in white and reddish-brown, a shade that reminded her of the color of Texas dirt. On the front of the shirts was the logo of the high school rodeo association. The back spelled out the names of all the teenage competitors.

Hanging on the wooden booth walls were denim jackets embroidered with horses, an outline of the state of Texas and other Western scenes. Adorned with sequins and beads, the shirts, hats and purses were like works of art. And all in good taste. Which was why word of mouth had spread and Maggie's shop was so successful.

Taylor hoped the same thing would happen with her dude-ranch business. Thanks to Mitch, she had the start she'd hoped for. If only she'd been able to keep herself from falling in love with him.

"How's it going?" Maggie asked her.

"How's it going with you?"

Taylor turned the question back on her friend. She didn't want to talk about it and she wouldn't lie and say everything was fine. This was the last night of championships, and when the event was over, Mitch would leave. Or he would stay because of Jensen.

Either way, her heart would be the worse for wear.

Apparently she wasn't the only one with things on her mind. Taylor realized that Maggie hadn't answered her question. And she was no longer casually leaning against the booth post.

"Everything okay, Mags?" she asked.

Maggie was frowning into the distance. "Those girls," she said, huffing out an exasperated breath.

"What's Faith up to?"

"It's not just my daughter. She's with Kasey and Stacy O'Connor, and the three of them put together don't have the good sense God gave a grasshopper. Although they flit hither and yon like one. Those three manage to get into all kinds of trouble. What one doesn't think of, another one will."

"Yeah, but they have a good time together," Taylor said.

"Too good," the other woman said grimly.

"Where are they?" Taylor asked, scanning the crowd. "Do you see them?"

"Oh, yeah. I promised Grady I would keep an eye on his twins since they're always with Faith. The girls have strict orders to stay in sight of this booth or suffer dire consequences."

"And what would those be?" Taylor asked, raising one eyebrow.

Maggie smiled. "I hope we don't ever have to find out.

"You don't have anything in mind, do you?"

She shook her head and red curls danced around her face. "I just hoped the words *dire consequences* would scare the bejesus out of them enough to keep the gruesome threesome in line."

"What are they doing?" Taylor asked, searching the crowd again.

"First your sister bought them cotton candy, licorice and soda. Now she's doing a French braid for one of the twins—I can never tell those two girls apart."

"Yeah, that sounds like Jen. She likes kids."

"They seem to like her, too. But you'd think someone as smart as she is would know better than to feed them so much sugar."

"When it comes to kids, I don't think book smarts count," Taylor commented.

"I'm going to have to peel my child off the ceiling tonight. I don't even want to think about what will happen at Grady's house. Double trouble," she said, shaking her head. "I wonder if he can arrest her for contributing to the hyperactivity of a minor."

"I hope not. Jen wouldn't do well in jail," Taylor said wryly. "Unless she could defend herself with words. At least her mouth is a match for her big heart."

With a lot of love stored up, Taylor added silently. And she wasn't thinking about the girls. Mitch Rafferty would be on the receiving end of all that tucked-away love.

She'd heard her sister talking to him late into the night the previous evening. The murmur of their voices out by the pool had carried to her in her downstairs bedroom. Then they'd gone up to their rooms, separated by a bathroom that she knew firsthand wasn't big enough to discourage any hanky-panky from a determined man.

In the past few days, she hadn't seen much

of that determined man. Her guests had kept her hopping. Rodeo activities in addition to her sister had kept him busy. It was clear to Taylor that the two were an item again. And every time Taylor remembered seeing Jen in Mitch's arms, the wave of pain that roared through her stole her breath.

"I can tell from here that Kasey and Stacy are gaga over her." Suddenly Maggie frowned and her whole body tensed.

"What's wrong?"

"That man stopped to talk to the girls."

"Anyone you know?"

"Never saw him before," Maggie said, the words clipped and uneasy.

"Is that a problem?"

"I don't know. He caught my eye earlier tonight. Just now he deliberately walked over to them."

"Where?" Taylor asked.

"Third row of the bleachers," Maggie answered, pointing. "Just to the right of the Vern's Tractor Company sign on the pipe fencing. And to the left of Gunderson's Pet and Feed Center."

"I still don't see them."

"They're almost right smack-dab behind your banner advertising the Stevens's dude ranch."

Taylor nodded. "Okay. I've got them. I just spotted Faith's dark, curly head pop up."

"Little squirt can't hold still for a microsecond. And all that sugar doesn't help." Worry sanded the edges of her voice.

"Okay." Taylor bobbed and weaved, trying to see. "There. He just turned around. I don't recognize him, either."

"Between the two of us, we know everyone in these parts. I don't like it."

"He's probably just hitting on Jen. She can handle him. And if she can't, Mitch will."

"I guess. But I still don't like it. If he doesn't mosey off and mind his own business, I'm fixin' to be on him like sequins on an evening gown." Maggie started to open the door to her booth.

"Down, girl." Taylor saw Grady walk up the three bleacher steps toward the group. "I think reinforcements are on the way," she said.

Maggie nodded. "That stranger saw, too. Did you see how fast he took off when he noticed the sheriff moving in?"

When Taylor's gaze slid from Grady back to Jensen and the girls, she realized that the man had disappeared into the crowd. She couldn't see him anymore. "He's gone. Good."

"Triple that for me." Maggie let out a long breath as Grady sat down with the female foursome. "All right. He's settling in for his shift to keep them under surveillance."

"He probably has time now. There are only a few events left after intermission."

"I'm glad he's there." She shook her head as she scanned the crowd, a worried expression on her freckled face. "There was something weird about that guy. In fact, there's something weird about the rodeo this year."

"What do you mean?"

"Don't you feel it? Sort of déjà vu? As if the past is catching up?"

Taylor *had* felt it. She and Mitch had talked about it. Still she asked, "Why do you say that?"

Maggie brushed the curls away from her small face and tucked them behind her ears. "Since I agreed to sell the rodeo T-shirts along with my own stock, I've been able to sit here and watch the crowd."

"So?" But Taylor heard the nerves in her friend's tone.

"I feel as if I'm seeing faces from the past."

"Like who?"

"Jack Riley."

"Jack's here?" Taylor asked.

"No." The other woman vehemently shook

her head as if sheer force of will could keep that from being so. "I'm sure it wasn't him. But it's as if Mitch coming back has made us all think about ten years ago." A troubled expression pulled her eyebrows together and puckered her forehead. "Go ahead, tell me I'm crazy."

"Certifiable," Taylor said, struggling to keep from grinning. "Any minute eerie stalker music will come over the PA system. Can the resident slasher be far behind? Watch your back, Mags."

The other woman held up her hand, and a sheepish smile turned up the corners of her mouth. "Okay. I get the point. But tell me you haven't looked at people in a crowd and spotted someone who was a dead ringer for a person you know. Only it wasn't them."

"Never happened to me," Taylor said, shaking her head.

"Okay. Be that way. But I've had that feeling tonight. I keep seeing this guy."

"You mean the one talking to the girls?"

Maggie shook her head. "Another guy. He's bigger and broader, more filled out, but he's got the same black hair and blue eyes as Jack Riley."

"Couldn't just be wishful thinking? Did

you have a crush on Jack that no one knew about?" Taylor suggested.

"No way," Maggie said, flatly denying it. "My parents forbade me to see 'wild' Jack. Do I have idiot written on my forehead?"

Taylor pretended to closely study her friend's small, heart-shaped face. "Nope. And even if it was, the curls would hide it."

"Curls I passed on to my daughter," her friend said, ruefully tucking her hair behind her ears again.

In spite of her close friendship with the other woman, Maggie had never named Faith's father, at least not to Taylor. But she knew if the man's name had passed Maggie's lips, it would be all over Destiny. The little girl had been conceived a decade ago, probably right around the championships. After all these years, Maggie and Faith were a package deal, a family. She'd come a long way from teenage mother to confident businesswoman who supported her daughter without help from anyone. Now it didn't really matter who had fathered Faith. But Taylor couldn't help being curious.

"How can you be sure this guy isn't Jack?" Taylor wanted to know.

"It's been ten years. Why would he come back now? Why after all this time?"

"Because Mitch is back."

"So he's a cosmic catalyst?"

Taylor smiled, but her gaze settled on her sister in the bleachers. A catalyst for calamity. "Jen is back, too," she said quietly.

Maggie's gaze swung back to the bleachers. "Yeah. And look how close Grady is sitting to her."

Taylor had noticed. Knowing Mitch, he would have something to say about that. "I guess he's as close as sequins on an evening dress," Taylor commented, using her friend's analogy as she tried to joke.

"That's not exactly the analogy I would use in reference to a hunk like Grady O'Connor. But if body language is anything to go by, he's doing surveillance on Jen as well as the gruesome threesome. Any closer and they'd be doing the wild thing."

"You do have a way with words, Mags."

"And the way Jen is smiling, she doesn't seem to be minding a bit. Do you think she's finally over Zach?"

"I suspect she is. But I don't think it's because of Grady."

"Then who?"

"Mitch."

Her friend studied her closely. "I can tell by the look on your face that's not a good thing."

"I'm not sure about the look on my face.

But no one would be happier than me if Jen found love again."

"As long as it was someone besides Mitch."

"I didn't say that," Taylor protested.

"You didn't have to. Has anyone ever told you everything you're thinking is written all over your face?"

"I don't know. But even if you're right, there are two reasons why it won't work."

"Lay them on me."

"Number one, I would never do anything to undermine my sister's happiness. I was afraid she was destined to be alone and I'm glad she's not."

"Even if it means you are?" Maggie asked pointedly.

Taylor shrugged. "I've got my business. Thanks to Mitch, I've got enough bookings for the year to actually make a profit. And most of the rodeo board of directors have said they're going to come back again. Repeat business is the key to success."

"I won't even go to where you sidestepped my actual question. What's the number two reason why being with Mitch won't work for you?"

Briefly Taylor considered avoiding the question. But she'd learned something about redheads. The red hair was traditionally an indicator of ferocious temper, which Maggie had. What was relatively unknown was the notorious redheaded persistence. She knew Maggie Benson wouldn't let it drop. In fact it was highly likely that she would bring it up at the most embarrassing moment possible.

"If you must know," Taylor said, "he rejected me once ten years ago because he was in love with my sister."

"And ten years ago she eloped with Zach Adams. Fight for him."

"It's not particularly smart to fight a losing battle. I just found out he's still in love with her."

Maggie touched her arm. "Oh, Taylor—"

"Don't," she said, holding up a hand. "If you're nice to me, I'll cry and I may not be able to stop. Jen's had enough unhappiness in her life. If she's happy now, I'm happy for her."

A sudden crackling sound filled the night air, but it cut in and out.

Maggie shook her head in disgust. "This rodeo has gone off without a hitch, except for Cal White's close call and that lousy PA system. I haven't been able to understand most of what comes over it."

"Folks…break." Mitch was making an announcement.

Taylor begrudged the fact that she knew it was him in spite of the fact it was only two discernible words.

"Bull riding...pro. Demonstration... Center arena...with me."

Taylor tensed, her stomach knotting with fear. "Did you understand any of that?" she asked her friend.

Maggie shrugged. "Sounded like Mitch is planning to demonstrate professional bull riding."

"That's what I thought, too. And I'm guessing that he'll get on one to do that," Taylor said grimly.

"Yeah." The other woman folded her arms over her chest.

"Damn it." Taylor's heart pounded painfully in her chest. "I have to talk to that stubborn, stupid, crazy fool," she said.

"Don't hurt him, Taylor."

"When I get through with him, he'll wish he'd taken his chances with the bull."

Maggie grinned. "I'll see you later."

Taylor hurried past the food concession. Around her the crowd dimmed and lights were a blur as she focused on one thing—getting to Mitch. To stop him from taking on a ton of trouble.

Was the man completely insane? Or was he

insanely jealous? Had he seen Jen and Grady sitting together in the bleachers? Was history repeating itself? Was his nose out of joint, as it had been ten years ago?

This time he would be taking the chance of doing more damage to his already injured leg, possibly losing it. Already weakened, it would be even more difficult for him to ride a bull. Not to mention the fact that he hadn't competed for years. He was out of practice.

Taylor hadn't been able to leave him alone ten years ago because she was frightened for him. Déjà vu all over again. Now she was terrified for the man she loved.

Chapter Twelve

Standing just outside the main arena, Mitch waited for any of the teenage riders to show up for his impromptu workshop. Bull riding was the last event. While they waited for the arena to be smoothed out for the intervening competitions, he thought he could give some pointers. But he wasn't sure anyone had heard. The damn PA system hadn't been working right all night. He wasn't sure his mike had broadcast intelligible information through the speakers.

He tapped the small electronic device clipped to his collar. Nothing. Then he looked at the power pack on his belt. It looked as if it was on, but no one had responded to his announcement.

Then he saw Taylor coming toward him. Her sun-streaked brown hair fell around her face like a silk curtain. Her confident stride swayed her hips in a completely fascinating, feminine and tantalizing way. And she looked as if she had a bone to pick with him.

God it was good to see her. There were so many things he wanted to tell her, but he hadn't had time. When his job was finished, he'd planned to find her. Now here she was. He didn't know what he'd done, but if it brought her to him, he would keep doing it. Forever.

His heart soared like a hot-air balloon. He loved her. Like a ton of ticked-off bul, the thought slammed him in the chest. He'd been hung up on two four-letter words—*love* and *home*.

Both were what he wanted more than anything.

Somehow, seeing Jen and hearing her say he was okay had knocked down the last emotional barrier built by a kid who had been let down one too many times. It wasn't her job to tell him he was all right, but it worked for him. Or maybe he was just grasping at straws, any truth that would give him the courage he needed to tell Taylor how much he loved her and wanted a life with her.

He'd told her once that when he figured out what he wanted, she'd be the first to know. Now was the time. He couldn't stand not knowing if she felt the same about him. Wine, flowers and that expensive dinner would have to wait.

She stopped in front of him, her breath coming in gasps from the furious pace she'd set.

"What are you trying to do?" she demanded.

"Get my act together," he answered.

"Well, you have a darned funny way of showing it."

"I don't know," he said, scratching his head. "It seemed like a good idea to me."

And about time he told her how he felt. He had to remember to thank Dev for twisting his arm to bring him back to Destiny. Otherwise he never would have figured things out.

"Are you crazy? You have no business doing this."

He frowned. What the hell was she talking about?

"Doing what?"

"Your leg, Mitch," she answered. "You haven't done this for a long time. It's a stupid idea."

"What?"

"Getting on a bull. What if you injure your leg again? You told me what the doctor said. You could lose it. Or if you get your head bashed in—" Her voice caught and she stopped. When she was in control again, she said, "It's an awfully hard head, but I'd say a ton of bull has you on size and strength."

She believed he was going to ride a bull? Then another idea struck him. She was worried about him. He'd swear she was. And he hoped that meant what he thought it did.

"How would you feel if I did get my head stomped on?" he asked, carefully watching her reaction.

The spotlights overhead caught the sheen of tears in her eyes. "That's a stupid question," she said defiantly, but her mouth trembled. Then she turned away.

"I don't think it's stupid. Tell me."

She shook her head and wouldn't look at him.

"I don't believe the gutsy girl I knew ten years ago has lost her gumption. Since when are you afraid to say what's on your mind?"

The barb spun her around to face him. "You want to know how I would feel?" Angrily she brushed at the single tear coursing down her cheek. "You need to know how I feel. No," she amended. She tapped her chest. "*I* need to tell you how I feel."

"Okay."

"Life is too short to leave things unsaid.

There are too many loose ends. They'll trip you up if you're not careful."

"Okay." He wished she would say it already. If she didn't, he would.

"I may be crazy for loving you, but it's true nonetheless."

Finally. He let out the breath he hadn't realized he'd been holding. He had the urge to pump his arm in victory. He was about to tell her what was on his mind, but she wasn't finished yet.

"I'm a one-man woman. You were always number one to me. I loved you ten years ago and I still do. I never stopped. I couldn't, no matter how hard I tried."

"You tried to stop loving me?"

"You bet I did."

"Why?"

"Because I knew you wanted Jen. And you still do."

"Hold it—"

She continued as if he hadn't spoken. "The day she came back, I saw you kiss her and hold her. She's what you want and I can't be anything but what I am."

"Wait—"

"It's okay, Mitch. I'll learn to live with it. Now that I got it off my chest, I feel a lot better." But more tears trickled down her cheeks, putting the lie to her bravado.

"Don't cry, sweetheart." Mitch cupped her face in his hands and brushed the tears away with his thumbs. Then he pulled her into his arms.

Struggling to push him away, Taylor hit the square pack hooked to his belt. "Don't, Mitch."

"Don't what? Care about you?" He rested his chin on the top of her head. "Too late. I already do. I love you." He smiled when he felt her arms go around him. "Jen and I will never be more than friends—except maybe brother- and sister-in-law. I can't believe you didn't know the kisses we shared were the forever after kind. You're the woman I want, Taylor. A home and a couple of kids would be nice, too. But as long as I've got you, nothing else really matters."

"I can't believe it," she said, sniffling. Keeping her hands at his waist, she took a half step back and met his gaze.

"Believe it. It's always been you and me. Ten years ago, you were the only one who wanted me, and I was so stupid that I pushed you away. Then I ran as fast as I could from the memories."

"But they were bad—"

He shook his head. "Not all of them. Not the ones about you."

"But Jen—"

"Is a good friend. Seeing her again helped me to put the past to rest. I will always be grateful to her."

"For what?"

"For making me realize how much I love you."

She blinked. Her heart was too full. But she had to ask. "How?"

"I wasn't jealous," he said as if that explained everything.

"And your point is?"

"I saw her with Grady and it didn't bother me a bit." He thought she relaxed slightly. "But every time I saw you with another guy, no matter how innocent, I wanted to clobber someone."

"You had no reason to be jealous."

"Why? Tell me, Taylor."

"I already did."

"Say it again," he demanded. "I need to hear it again."

"I love you, Mitch." Her words echoed weirdly in the night air but all she could think about was Mitch.

As Taylor stared into his blue eyes, she heard the crowd start to chant. The noise grew louder and it was several moments before she realized that over and over they were saying, "Kiss her."

"Now the damn thing works." Mitch glared at the grinning spectators in the grandstand, then took her hand and led her to a quiet corner on the other side of the barn.

Frowning, he flicked the microphone, then flipped a switch on the gizmo hooked to his belt to shut it off.

"I think it worked just fine," she said, smiling up at him. "When you made your announcement, the static made it sound like you were going to ride a bull. That's what made me find you. To try to talk you out of doing something dumb."

She remembered thinking that not even a bull could drag out of her how she felt about him. She'd been wrong.

"I'm finally getting smart." He ripped the mike off and dropped it. Then he pulled her into his arms. Lowering his head, he pressed his mouth to hers.

Several moments later, he broke the kiss and whispered, "Marry me, Taylor. I want to spend the rest of my life with you making you happy."

"But, Mitch," she said, "you're leaving

after the rodeo. My life, my roots are here on the ranch. I can't go."

"I didn't ask you to," he said. "And you didn't ask me to stay." His lips turned up in a smile that was sexy, and wonderful, and hopeful.

"Would you? Stay here with me?" she invited. "I know Destiny doesn't have the best memories for you. But—"

He put his finger over her lips to silence her. "No buts. The only memories that count for me are of you and they're here. I can do business anywhere. But I can't live without you. I'll be happy as long as we're together, even if we live in a cardboard box under a cottonwood tree. The rest will fall into place."

She rested her cheek against his chest and snuggled into his arms. "I guess it's not true what they say."

"What's that?"

"You *can* go home again. Maybe that's because you can't escape Destiny."

He laughed. "I've run away from it long enough. The town and the truth."

"And what is the truth, Mitch?"

"My destiny is loving you."

"And mine is loving you right back," she said.

Destiny? Fate? Karma? She didn't know

what to call it. But she was more grateful than she could say for whatever force had returned Mitch Rafferty to her arms.

* * * * *

YES! Please send me the *Cowboy at Heart* collection in Larger Print. This collection begins with 3 FREE books and 2 FREE gifts in the first shipment, and more free gifts will follow! My books will arrive in 8 monthly shipments until I have the entire 51-book *Cowboy at Heart* collection. I will receive 2 or 3 FREE books in each shipment and I will pay just $4.99 U.S./ $5.89 CDN. for each of the other four books in each shipment, plus $2.99 for shipping and handling.* If I decide to keep the entire collection, I'll have paid for only 32 books because 19 books are FREE! I understand that by accepting the 3 free books and gifts places me under no obligation to buy anything. I can always return a shipment and cancel at any time. My free books and gifts are mine to keep no matter what I decide.

256 HCN 0779   456 HCN 0779

Name _____ (PLEASE PRINT) _____

Address _____ Apt. # _____

City _____ State/Prov. _____ Zip/Postal Code _____

Signature (if under 18, a parent or guardian must sign)

Mail to the **Harlequin® Reader Service:**
IN U.S.A.: P.O. Box 1867, Buffalo, NY 14240-1867
IN CANADA: P.O. Box 609, Fort Erie, Ontario L2A 5X3

* Terms and prices subject to change without notice. Prices do not include applicable taxes. Sales tax applicable in N.Y. Canadian residents will be charged applicable taxes. This offer is limited to one order per household. All orders subject to approval. Credit or debit balances in a customer's account(s) may be offset by any other outstanding balance owed by or to the customer. Please allow 4 to 6 weeks for delivery. Offer available while quantities last. Offer not available to Quebec residents.

Your Privacy—The Harlequin® Reader Service is committed to protecting your privacy. Our Privacy Policy is available online at www.ReaderService.com or upon request from the Harlequin Reader Service.

We make a portion of our mailing list available to reputable third parties that offer products we believe may interest you. If you prefer that we not exchange your name with third parties, or if you wish to clarify or modify your communication preferences, please visit us at www.ReaderService.com/consumerschoice or write to us at Harlequin Reader Service Preference Service, P.O. Box 9062, Buffalo, NY 14269. Include your complete name and address.

CAHBPA13

ReaderService.com

Manage your account online!

- Review your order history
- Manage your payments
- Update your address

*We've designed
the Harlequin® Reader Service
website just for you.*

Enjoy all the features!

- Reader excerpts from any series
- Respond to mailings and
  special monthly offers
- Discover new series available to you
- Browse the Bonus Bucks catalog
- Share your feedback

Visit us at:
ReaderService.com